I0750519

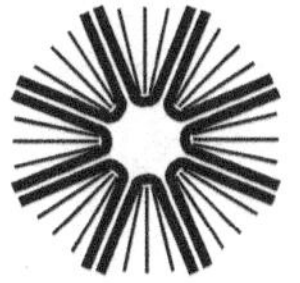

SCHOOLGIRL

SCHOOLGIRL

followed by **BAD MUSIC**

by Rie Qudan

translated from the Japanese
by Haydn Trowell

GAZEBO BOOKS SUMMER HILL 2025

Gazebo Books
PO Box 375
Summer Hill
New South Wales 2130
Australia
gazebobooks.com.au

First Japanese edition published by Bungeishunju Ltd., in 2022
First published in English translation by Gazebo Books, 2025

This English edition published by arrangement with Bungeishunju Ltd., Tokyo in care of Tuttle-Mori Agency, Inc., Tokyo

Grateful acknowledgement is made to Allison Markin Powell for permission to quote from her translation of *Schoolgirl* by Osamu Dazai, published by One Peace Books, copyright 2011.

National Library of Australia
Cataloguing-in-Publication Entry
Author: Rie Qudan
Schoolgirl
ISBN 978 1 7636009 2 8 (paperback)

Cover image: *Ko-omote* mask by Hideta Kitazawa. Photography by Sohta Kitazawa. Courtesy of the artist and the photographer.

Cover and interior design by Mountains Brown Press.

SCHOOLGIRL

A dream. I'm dreaming.

I'm standing in my kitchen at home, a deluge of ingredients laid out before me on the kitchen bench. Huge chunks of meat, the kind you would normally find only in large restaurants. Dozens of fish, too big to hold in my hands, all facing the same direction. Vegetables, fruits, canned foods, even jars of seasonings. But they're all larger than they ought to be. A mind-numbing abundance of choices. Yet I'm already busy trying to figure out which ingredients to select, which parts to cut, what combinations to prepare, what would give my daughter the biggest smile. That's when she arrives home – and when I notice her changed appearance, I realise this is no time for cooking. Her body is like a sketch someone stopped drawing halfway through, small details that ought to be there inexplicably missing. Her left eye is a hollow cavity, her right ear nowhere to be seen. Her left arm is absent, and so too is her right leg, as if to compensate for the imbalance.

My daughter has been reduced by half. Halved due to some unfathomable law of nature. In my dreams, I'm unusually perceptive. My mind is clearer now than it has ever been awake. The law of half-daughters. I'm already aware that for every paired body part, one half is missing. I can tell it's all a dream, that none of this is real. And yet the dream keeps on going. A dream. I'm dreaming. I have to be. Again and again, I try to rouse myself, to tell the dream I've caught on. But it refuses to listen, the strange scene continuing without end. I can't wake up.

Trapped in this bizarre situation, and yet finding myself unnaturally composed, I look for a switch, something, anything to turn my daughter back to normal. As I wade through the various foodstuffs, a mechanical voice sounds from overhead: 'Each of the internal organs has been reduced by half. The kidneys by half. The ovaries by half. The blood by half. The bone marrow by half.' Then, with a stiff smile and a pale countenance that looks to have been overly processed by some smartphone photography app, my daughter says to me: 'I'm home, Mum.'

I snap awake. My daughter is gone.

Waking up in the morning is always interesting.

'Once upon a time, there I was.' When I was a girl, I liked to talk about my moods after waking up in the morning, and it was with those words that my stories always began. I had a close friend I could talk to about anything and everything. And we did talk, endlessly, until I had emptied my mind of all the stray thoughts popping into my head. About how not having a father so often brought me to the verge of tears. About how I did have a mother, so incredibly important to me, for whom I would do just about anything. I told my friend everything, from what I didn't like about my own face, to the mean streak I tried to keep secret from everyone else, to the embroidery on my underwear. And she did the same with me. There were no secrets between us.

When I wake up in the mornings, my body still unformed, having melted into the warmth of my blankets – especially those mornings after waking from a grotesque nightmare – I like to look back on the rambling stories that we used to share back then. It makes me want to go back to sleep, to immerse myself in distant memories and turn my mind back to that girl I was so close to. Because for that brief, fleeting moment, I can turn back time. I can return to a moment when the door was still only hanging slightly ajar, a thin sliver of light peeking in. I'll stand there on my tiptoes, blindfolded on the boundary line, perched so that the slightest breeze – even something as slight as the flapping of a butterfly's wings – could push me forward, stumbling from the outside into the world of my dreams, and this time, I'm sure they'll be good ones. I'll forget all other thoughts, pulling forth only those happy feelings from a time back when every morning was filled with fun. And I'll say to her that the morning is grey, and I'll blush with awkward embarrassment in the hazy light. And she'll understand me completely. Yes, when you open the box, you find another box waiting inside. One box, another box, another again. It goes on and on, but in the end, there's nothing. It's empty. Which one of us started talking about boxes? After that, we spoke of emptiness. She must have been the one who brought it up. Emptiness. Next, it was glasses. And from glasses, we turned to eyes, and…and?

I don't know. What exactly was fun about waking up in the morning again? Here I am, racked by a familiar headache and a parched throat, my heart still racing from the shock of the nightmare – and of course, this uneasy feeling in the pit of my stomach, like I've forgotten something dreadfully important. There's nothing fun here. Nothing at all.

I pry my eyelids open. Dim-coloured waves scatter in my eyes before coalescing into light. Pulled free from my blanket, my body is cold. Now then, today. Tomorrow, as of yesterday. The tomorrow that yesterday I believed would inevitably dawn. And here it is. I come back to myself. I remember everything. That she never was, this close friend of mine. Unfortunately, I've never had any real friends I could share my secrets with. The girl I remembered just now was a product of the mind, an imaginary friend I created in my childhood. Now, all I have is my daughter. But there's so much to do. I have to prepare breakfast. In the kitchen, I fill the kettle with water and switch it on. Since bringing her into this world, not a day has gone by that I've forgotten to prepare breakfast for her. Not a day. Like cards lying face down on the table flipping over one by one, my surroundings start to come back into focus, and this time, I wake up fully.

'AI? What time is it?'

'It's 7.45 am.'

So begins the calm male voice. As though he has been waiting for us humans to rouse from our beds, to set loose the bounty of information gathered during the course of the night. The face of a clean-looking news announcer in a necktie and a navy suit comes to mind. I made the right call changing the default settings from the young woman's voice last night. The man's lower frequencies are more soothing to my ears. He reads back the message from my husband, which came in during the early hours of the morning, purple light flickering on the smooth-textured vessel in which he's housed. My husband won't be coming home today, either. It seems his flight last night was cancelled. AI, putting two and two together, tactfully recites the latest information extracted from the French airline's website.

'Stop,' I say, and he promptly instructs me to clean the air purifier and notifies me of a new video uploaded on *Awakenings*. Next, suggestions for breakfast: 'How about a *komatsuna*, banana, and soymilk smoothie? Or miso soup with *komatsuna* and *abura-age*? You should use the *komatsuna* soon.'

I set out to cook breakfast, following his instructions. After a while, I realise it's because the room is so dim that my vision seems darker than usual. I glance outside the window, and one of the sources of my uneasiness after waking up this morning is made clear. Placing the *komatsuna* I was about to wash in a colander, I stumble forward and open the window.

'Today is the first day of July,' sounds the report behind me as a strong gale roars in my face.

July. Only six months left in the year. Just as I think how much of a hassle it will be to plan a trip to see my mother around New Year's, I find myself breaking out into an amused smile at an uplifting suggestion: 'Why not start something new today?' The smart speaker was only delivered the other day, so I only really had a chance to play around with the voice settings a little, but I had never before used one that seemed so warm and caring during its initial setup. *Positivity*, as my daughter called it in English – endeavouring to be always helpful and considerate – was the latest trend in AI personalities, it seemed. I wasn't used to its presence yet, but no doubt I would quickly adapt to this cutting-edge piece of technology intended to enrich its users' lives. Give it a month, and I might even start feeling uncomfortable using older models, which lacked this distinctive blend of positivity.

The balcony is covered, so the sheets that I had hung out to dry haven't gotten overly wet. I roll the cold, damp cloth around my arms and throw it into the living room, yet I remain outside. Perhaps the wind will help ease my headache. Placing my hands on the balcony railing, I crane my neck to stare up overhead. Countless lines of water are pouring from somewhere far beyond that monotonous, leaden sky, only to be sucked straight into the ground like the earnest love of an innocent young girl. Something is clearly wrong with me this morning, with the word 'love' suddenly springing to mind like that.

Is it a universal phenomenon, for there to be drizzling rain whenever something sad happens? But when I focus on the sound of the rain like this, what I feel is more anger than sadness. Yes, rain is definitely an apt metaphor for tears. In fact, the first scene this particular rain brings to mind is a childhood memory, an old fear of mine that I too would turn into rain if I let myself cry too long. Even when I screamed so loudly it felt like my throat was going to tear itself apart, no one would notice me, my voice drowned out by the pouring rain. First, I would lose the ability to tell the difference between my tears, my runny nose, and the heavy drops hitting me on the face, and that feeling would gradually move down my body, until finally it assimilated everything, all the way to the soles of my feet, and I would disappear into the downpour without a trace. Terrified by my own horrible fantasies, I would bite the inside of my cheeks with all my strength to force myself to stop crying, but still I wouldn't be able to stem the tears from spilling out one after the other. At such times, it would be my dear friend who came to cheer me up. She was such a kind girl. 'Your mother doesn't really mean to hit you,' she would say to comfort me.

'You're always poking at things better left untouched. So let's go tell her you'll be good from now on. Try to imagine how she must be feeling. You need to treasure your mother.' She would always have words of encouragement for me. 'Be a good daughter. Cherish your mother.' Always such wonderful ideas.

But now, I just can't bring myself to accept those sugar-coated suggestions. Today, I find myself wondering why exactly I should cherish my mother. Now, I find my friend's misguided kindness grating. Offensive.

She has a kind soul – there's no doubt about that – but she's so out of touch with the real world, so old-fashioned in her thinking. Her values are those of a century past, stuck in the pre-war era, like the anachronistic monologue of some doddering politician, going on and on about how children ought to serve their parents without question. They haven't been updated in decades. If you found a child locked outside their home and left to cry in the rain in this day and age, you would call the police. You wouldn't spout some nonsense about cherishing your mother. Everyone knows that. So why didn't they? Why didn't they? The pelting rain fills my heart only with anger and animosity.

I finish making breakfast and go to call my daughter. She's sitting at her study desk. She often edits her videos during the morning hours, her right leg crossed over her left one, her right hand moving the mouse back and forth while the fingers of her left hand type away at the keyboard. Though she may have a growing posture problem from too much time spent staring at computer and tablet screens, her body is whole. All the necessary organs, the blood, the bones, are right where they should be in any fourteen-year-old girl. She looks no different than yesterday, yet the sight of her strikes me as brand new, so fresh that if you told me she had only just been assembled this very morning, I would probably believe you. And so I inform the girl with her flawless, pristine body that breakfast is ready.

A short while later, my daughter steps into the living room and gulps down the soymilk smoothie I prepared for her. Then, she stares across at the bacon and eggs waiting for her at the kitchen table.

'I told you, I don't eat bacon. Or eggs, either,' sounds a hoarse voice.

By now, we've repeated this exchange so many times I know exactly where the conversation is headed. I retreat to the dressing room in the back, pretending not to hear her. But my daughter must be in a temper this morning, as she keeps on listing the various reasons why she won't eat bacon, eggs, or any other animal-derived foods. Before I know it, it's like someone has flicked a switch, and the sounds flowing from my daughter's lips are no longer Japanese, but English, words like *greenhouse gases*, *animal rights*, and *speciesism* pouring out one after the next. I was already acting as if I couldn't hear her, but now I well and truly can't understand what she's saying. I'm an outsider, a stranger to this brave new language system. My daughter knows I can't keep up when she uses complicated English, but she makes no effort to lower the level of her vocabulary and grammar.

I pause while taking the washing out of the dryer, thinking for a moment that I heard the word *kōrisugi* – too frozen. Wondering whether the broccoli I used in the salad wasn't thawed properly, I make my way back to the door and peek through the crack into the living room.

'*Kōrisugi*?' my voice whispers.

'Not *su*.'

'What?'

'Not *su*. *Shu*.'

'*Shu*?'

'*Shū-gi*,' the girl repeats, emphasising the *shu* in a way that sounds closer to the English word *shoe*.

'*Shūgi*?'

'*Shu-gi*.'

'What's a *shu-gi*?'

'*Kōri-shugi*.'

I sort through the dry laundry, unable to make sense of my daughter's words still echoing in my mind. As I stack the underwear from dark to light, she continues to mutter under her breath. Eventually, a low voice sounds from behind the door: 'You're such an airhead, Mum,' it says in perfect Japanese. It's plain from the effort she put into the pronunciation that she wants me to hear it loud and clear.

Leaving the dressing room and making my way through my daughter's room and into the walk-in closet in the main bedroom, where all the clothes are stored, it suddenly hits me. *Shugi*. 'Doctrine.' An -ism. That's what she was trying to say.

'Ma-ma.'

It seemed like yesterday that my daughter formed her first meaningful words, bringing her upper and lower lips, like radiant rose petals, together to say 'Ma-ma'. For the longest while, that one repeated syllable monopolised her speech. 'Ma-ma.' It's hard to believe that fourteen years later, it's been replaced by something as elaborate as an -ism.

I can't say whether *kōri-shugi* was supposed to mean 'frozenism' or 'utilitarianism', but it was almost certainly some sort of -ism. Maybe she meant it as a disparagement? I understand at some vague level that my daughter is much smarter than I am. She thinks much more deeply, much further ahead than I did at fourteen, and comes out with ideas that wouldn't even occur to her father. She's already grown up. She'll be fine. In the darkness of the closet, I sink down to the floor, overcome with emotion as I reflect on the course of my daughter's journey thus far. The day is only just beginning, and already I'm crying my eyes out, like someone looking back with a sense of accomplishment on a hard day's work. 'My life has been for her sake,' I think, coming right out with some corny, overly dramatic line. Yes, I'm glad I had her. Here I am, finally joining the ranks of mothers the world over unabashedly proclaiming how happy they are to have children. If someone were to write a novel about my life, if I were the protagonist, this moment here would be the final scene. I don't want any further developments. 'Congratulations.' 'Congratulations.' Those words of blessing I heard in the delivery room fourteen years ago when I first glimpsed my daughter through blurry eyes come rushing back. I've won the battle. I'm the hero returning home after a successful mission. The sun is rising high, burning bright, all but implying the tale ends on a happy note. A satisfied expression. Beautiful music. A long credits sequence. The curtain falls.

'Money. I need to charge my Suica card for the train.'

My daughter's voice, sounding behind two separate walls, prompts me to sit up straight. I check my wallet, only to find that I'm short on 1,000-yen and 5,000-yen bills. I pull out a 10,000-yen bill and hand it to her. My daughter shoves it into her skirt pocket.

'You'll hurt the money if you handle it like that,' I say. 'Look after it in your wallet. That note has to be tired, given how much travelling it must have done during its life. It doesn't deserve to be treated roughly.'

My daughter snickers, but she still doesn't put the money away properly. Standing in front of the full-length mirror at the entrance, she starts gathering her waist-length hair to tie back into a bundle. Like mine, her hair has a tendency to swell in humid conditions until it becomes all but impossible to manage, but she insists she needs to grow it another two centimetres to donate it to charity. In a mere two months, her hair from the neck down will in all likelihood grace the head of a child undergoing cancer treatment. If I close my eyes, I can readily imagine my daughter's hair bringing a smile to the face of a child in a cancer ward. It isn't necessarily a joyful image, but it isn't a sad one, either.

'Use the money carefully, okay? Don't give it to those people doing fundraisers in front of the station. Your father's company already makes plenty of donations. Use that 10,000-yen note for your train fare and to buy a drink, okay?'

'What organisations?'

'Hmm?'

'Dad's company. What organisations does it donate to?'

'Organisations…? Hmm?' I stammer, clamming up. 'Charitable organisations, of course. Yes, like environmental…environmental issues. Or protecting… human rights? SDGs? That sort of thing.'

'Yeah, so which ones? What are they called? Which environmental issues? Specifically? You're just saying whatever comes to mind, aren't you? You don't know what you're talking about. Do your research before you make stuff up.'

My daughter heaves a gloomy sigh, acting for all the world like an old man with only a few short years left to live, then shakes her head in a decidedly un-Japanese manner.

'Do you know where the money from Dad's company is *actually* going, Mum? It's just a *performance* to them. They're hypocrites. If you Google it, the answer comes up right away. Not a single yen reaches those who really need the donations. Not one.'

'It doesn't?'

'No. You don't even know that? It's just *greenwashing*, what Dad's company does. How can you be so laidback all the time, Mum? I bet you think so long as you can live in comfort, everything's fine. You don't even realise how filthy the world is, how everything's controlled and manipulated. My generation is going to pay the price for you clueless adults just going about doing whatever you want. Wake up, already. The world's falling apart, and you don't even know it. It's so bad I don't even know how to keep on living.'

As I focus on the fluid movements of my daughter's lips, the sight before me begins to seem less and less like something I can reach out and touch with my fingers. I feel like I'm simultaneously looking back at a past memory and experiencing a virtual reality vision of the near future. I don't know when it is, exactly, but there she is, my daughter from some unknown time. Filled with anticipation and a sense of premonition, I see her not with my eyes, but in my mind, an illusion muddied with reality. Who is this stubborn girl calling me 'Mum'? I'm not her Mum. Just her Ma-ma.

Feeling like I'm about to be swallowed up whole by my stray imaginings, I manage to squeeze out the words: 'Come straight home today. Make sure you're back by seven. It sounds like your father won't be home tonight, either, so let's go out for dinner, just the two of us.'

'I can't. I'm going to study outside after class.'

'Outside? At Starbucks? Wouldn't it be easier to study at home?'

'Shut up. I'm not your property.'

With her signature phrase, delivered crisply and definitively, my daughter strides out the front door. Then, after one final English sentence that I can't begin to make sense of sounds back, the door closes.

Hi guys, welcome back to my channel. *Konnichiwa*. Thanks for watching *Awakenings*. Are you all awake?

So, er, I've kind of started speaking in Japanese all of a sudden… I had a feeling something like this would happen, but actually doing it…it's kind of embarrassing, I guess. But this time, I decided I wanted to do a video in Japanese, so that's what I'll do. My cheeks are getting all red here… I might sound a little strange until I get into the swing of things, but let's just see how we go.

I mainly use Japanese at home, when talking to my mum. My dad works for an overseas company, so I can usually get through to him in English, but I mostly speak with my mum in basic Japanese. I live in Tōkyō, but I don't really have many opportunities to speak it. I've been going to international schools since kindergarten, and the tutor I've been seeing this year is English, too. Even my Japanese friends speak English with me, so Japanese is just kind of something I learn at school and use with my mum. What I'm trying to say is it feels really weird speaking it alone in front of a camera while she's not around.

My mum, you know, she's super *shy*. She doesn't work. She doesn't like meeting new people. All she ever does is stay home reading books. So basically, when I think about Japanese, I've always got this *shy* image of it. It's like the meaning surrounding the words is always swirling around, always weak and ambiguous... Like you can't get to the centre of it, like you're just collecting vague hints or brief glimpses. I feel like I'm trying to imagine what a live concert's like just by the sound leaking outside. It's that kind of feeling. I don't think English is *shy*, though – it's firmer, more direct and straightforward. So when I hear myself speaking in Japanese, I can't help but think I lack confidence. My friends say I'm like a totally different person when I use Japanese. It's true, I think your personality does change when you switch languages. Because when I'm not using my mum's language, I can be so much more assertive. Like it says in my profile, I consider myself a *utilitarian*, an *altruist*, a *vegetarian*, and a *realist*. In English, I can define myself. But when I'm speaking Japanese, like I am now, I feel like I'm just my mum's daughter. I'm not sure of myself. So for me, I don't really see Japanese as being suitable for these livestreams, not when I'm trying to address a large audience. It just doesn't really work.

Kōri-shugi.

In the silence of the empty room, the air taut and thin now that my daughter has left for school, I try imitating her voice.

Then, even though I haven't uttered the wake word… '*Kōri-shugi* – utilitarianism. An ethical philosophy that takes happiness and social utility as its standard of value, considering these to be the primary purpose of life,' the hyper-confident AI responds.

Even in Japanese, I can't grasp the explanation. I ask AI to elaborate, and he begins reading out parts from a website.

'Utilitarianism…'

At the washbasin, I lather the foaming net with soap while the speaker pours out one abstract word after another, then bury my face in the cleansing soap. 'Jeremy Bentham. The greatest good for the greatest number.' I rinse off the foam, then press my hands, soaked in moisturiser, against my face and count the seconds while it penetrates my skin. One, two, three… 'John Stuart Mill. Higher pleasures and lower pleasures.'

'Better to be a human being dissatisfied than a pig satisfied; better to be Socrates dissatisfied than a fool satisfied.'

AI quotes what sounds like an aphorism. Unable to make sense of the context before and after, the only concrete images that linger in my mind are of pigs, humans, and fools. My brain classifies pigs and fools into one group, while placing humans and Socrates into another. I meticulously apply the facial serum and moisturiser, each costing over 20,000 yen, onto my face. Then, I interrupt AI's ongoing explanation of utilitarianism and call into the living room: 'Play the most recent video from *Awakenings*.'

First the YouTube logo appears on the eighty-inch TV screen, followed by my daughter's face, magnified to two or three times its actual size. She looks restless, rubbing her collarbone area with one hand without looking directly at the camera, then starts talking about the Japanese language in Japanese.

I turn up the volume on the TV and go back to the bathroom to put on my makeup. Every time I hear my daughter say the word 'Mum', however, my body reacts instinctively, my hands pausing mid-action. Of course, she isn't calling out to me. She's simply talking about her mother to people she has never met before. Does she know her own mother watches these videos? Was she bringing up this topic on purpose to see how I would react? It occurs to me she may have hidden a private message in this latest episode, and my attention begins to wander. When I come to, I realise I've skipped a step in my makeup routine.

No, that isn't it. The hand gliding over my cheeks comes to a complete stop. All at once, the cosmetics in their round and square containers strike me as empty blocks, and I forget the roles assigned to each. I suffer from this kind of mild memory impairment from time to time, especially when I'm at home without the stabilising presence of my daughter. If she were within my line of sight, I wouldn't forget the functions of such simple objects. But in my current state, letting down my guard even for the briefest of moments means it's already too late. All tangible objects become mere forms devoid of meaning. I can make out the outlines of my own body, but I don't know whose it is to inhabit and move. The stitches holding my heart and body together unravel like a piece of ribbon.

A woman with a strange face, only the left side covered in skin-coloured powder, stares back at me in the mirror. If only she could have done something sooner about the right half of her face, I think. But now, she wants to die. She doesn't feel like finishing her makeup, nor anything else of the sort. Since she won't have to deal with other people once dead, there would be no need for her to bother applying makeup, either. With a dismissive air, she tries to hold her breath, to stop breathing once and for all. But death isn't something to be taken lightly, I tell her. Her wish for it all to end is simply the result of a chemical imbalance in her brain. She has a beautiful home with a spacious balcony, and her husband brings in so much money each month she doesn't have the faintest idea how to spend it. She gets along well with her husband's parents, and above all, her daughter is as bright as they come. She's blessed as a mother, and ought to be happier than she has any right to be. Really, she's in the top three per cent of human beings in that regard. She doesn't want to die. She just hasn't been sleeping well lately. She's tired, that's all.

'I'm tired,' she echoes obediently.

Then, like a sleepwalker, she stumbles away from the mirror. Realising just how exhausted she truly is, a sudden drowsiness comes over her, to the point that she can no longer manage to keep her eyes open. Even without vision, her body knows its way around the apartment and steps into the living room, the very room in which her daughter grew from a baby to her current gargantuan size. On the way, her leg strikes something with full force, sending a sharp jolt through the tips of her toes. It must have been her daughter's tablet, left charging at the power outlet near the floor. She may have scratched the outer case, but she doesn't care. She simply throws herself, body and mind, onto the sofa and lets herself sink down into the cushions. A high-pitched ringing, as of some electronic device malfunctioning, pierces her skull. 'You're such an airhead.' 'Shut up.' 'Wake up already.' The voice of the girl here with her until just a moment ago lingers in the air.

What would have happened, the woman wonders, if she had spoken out that way to her own mother when she was fourteen years old?

Her own mother would have probably smacked her over the head, then come out with a line like: 'How dare you speak to your parents that way!' Then, she would have left her standing outside as punishment. Yes, that's what she would have done. It was a well-known fact that there are two types of parents in the world: those who beat their children, and those who don't. Her mother belonged to the former group. With that thought, her mother's words as she casually beats her child sound anew. 'What are your eyes for?' her mother would demand if she didn't see what was expected of her. 'What are your ears for?' her mother would press if she didn't do what she was told. 'What is your mouth for?' her mother would bark if she remained silent. There were more, depending on the situation – head, hands, feet. Her mother, who couldn't maintain a modicum of sanity without constantly drowning herself in alcohol, had a disorder in the language processing area of her brain, and so would always use the same syntax when cursing her children. Though she tried to ignore them, the memories of her mother, always hitting her for one reason or another, flash again and again before the woman's eyes like a television advertisement on loop.

'You should leave soon to make your next calendar appointment. Shall I call a taxi?'

I open my eyes to a soothing voice – the calm voice of a man who has neither witnessed nor felt first-hand such acts of violence. Yes, I want to get the doctor's visit over with as quickly as possible so I can spend the afternoon cooking soup at home.

I rise to my feet, turn off the TV, and wash off the makeup covering half my face. I open the kitchen cupboard, take two cannabidiol tablets to calm my nerves, and wash them down with a glass of water. I put on my glasses, a shirt over my bra top, then a skirt with an elastic waistband. I place the untouched bacon and eggs in the refrigerator. I slip my feet into my sneakers. I open the door, when –

'Are you sure you don't need your phone?' AI shouts at maximum volume.

In the dim light, the red emergency LED ring on the smart speaker fills the room with an air of impalpable tension.

I guess I should explain why I'm speaking in Japanese, seeing how I said I don't think it's really suitable for serious discussion. Basically, the idea behind this channel is to inform people living privileged lives in advanced countries about dire situations happening all over the world. As I'm always saying, while you're sitting at home drinking your fruit juice and watching YouTube, the Earth's environment is under constant assault, and tens of thousands of people are dying from hunger every single day. To put it bluntly, if you think you're living a happy life free of inconvenience, you're stuck in a dream world. How can you claim to be living in reality when you only ever see the tiniest fraction of the world around you? I started *Awakenings* to wake people up from that blissful sleep. I'll be honest, it's the worst possible thing to have to open your eyes to, considering the world is filled with all this pain and suffering. But if people keep on ignoring the world as it is, it's only going to get worse. We, the younger generation, have to act – we have to do *something* about the negative legacy left behind by older generations. So won't you join me in trying to make the world a better place? If we can change people's awareness, we can change the future. Let's start a revolution. You know, there's a theory out there that man was born for love and revolution.

I've been getting all sorts of comments since I started posting these videos. To be honest, I never expected so many responses after just one month, so I'm really grateful. But I get the impression the people leaving comments and offering up words of encouragement are already invested in environmental and social issues, which is probably how they found this channel in the first place. But doesn't that make this just an echo chamber? You don't get anywhere just talking to people who already share the same values. Basically, I can't help but feel we're not reaching the people who really need to see this channel, the ones still indifferent to the actual state of the world. After giving it a lot of thought, I came to the conclusion I should target the Japanese demographic first. Which is why, for now, I'm planning to make more videos in Japanese and to expand my audience. I really want to get more people interested, so to my Japanese viewers, please share this with everyone you know. But at the same time, I feel like simply translating into Japanese while sticking to my usual approach won't be enough. Like I mentioned, most people who come across this channel are already awake, and the ones we really need to reach are still sound asleep. Repeating the same old story again and again won't get us anywhere.

A small display is mounted at eye level on the back of the headrest of the chair in front of me. I close my eyes to take a nap, but the flickering lights of advertisements pass through my eyelids, sparking my optic nerves. Around Mita or Azabu, a motorbike suddenly changes lanes in front of us, forcing the taxi to brake suddenly and the seatbelt to dig into my shoulder as gravity flings me forward. I feel like the main character in *A Clockwork Orange*, and a violent movie scene comes to life in my mind, filling me with nausea. Tied to a chair, my eyelids prised open with metal clips, forced to watch scene after scene to rehabilitate my mind and change me from bad to good.

Recently, my nightmares have become so severe I've decided to seek out therapy. The underlying cause remains unclear. It all started around ten days ago when I upgraded our AI smart speaker. My daughter, accusing me of being an 'unconscious consumer' after replacing our previous speaker less than six months after buying it, threw a fit and forced me to watch a certain video, a documentary produced by an overseas TV station covering the violence in the Democratic Republic of the Congo. Minerals used in electronic devices, including smartphones and computers, are mined throughout the country, and armed groups inflict all sorts of violence on local residents in order to monopolise those minerals. The programme featured women who had been sexually assaulted, providing visual evidence of violence my brain refused to imagine. Those gruesome images have kept me awake these past couple of weeks. I'm already prone to anxiety, so much so that films like *A Clockwork Orange* tend to leave me a nervous wreck. The real-life documentary was even more overwhelming.

Even when I open my eyes, the faces of those women, contorted in pain, are practically burned into my retinas. My daughter was right – I *am* an unconscious consumer. My convenient, comfortable life is built on their sacrifices. In exchange for my peaceful, dream-like reality, someone else is being subjected to an endless nightmare. Yes, everything my daughter said is true. I understand, intuitively, what she's trying to say – smartphones and the like ought to be eradicated from the face of the earth to free those people from the fear of violence. But reality is never the sort of thing to line up with your intuition. Just as cars will never disappear from the world in spite of the countless souls who perish in traffic accidents each and every day, so too are smartphones now a permanent fixture in society as we know it.

When I was a little girl, my intuition was often at odds with reality. 'Why?' I would ask my mum.

Never again would I ask her that question. Now, when I think of the word 'mum', it's myself I see, and I no longer question the word's myriad contradictions. On the rare occasion a question does arise, it isn't long before I forget it.

Even if I were to stop using smartphones altogether, it wouldn't change things in the slightest. And so, with that half-hearted excuse, I resume the unfinished video from earlier. My daughter, growing increasingly confident in her speaking, begins to explain why she created her YouTube channel. Having already heard all this in previous videos, I increase the playback speed by fifty percent. My daughter starts speaking rapidly, as if being chased by something, her gestures restless and unsettled. Just before she can begin expressing her dissatisfaction with her limited audience, however, the video stops, the connection probably impacted by the rain, and my daughter is reduced to a still image.

I log into Facebook while waiting for the stream to buffer. A friend from college has posted a photo of a book, accompanied by a lengthy paragraph. 'I haven't read many books these past few years,' it begins, gradually evolving into long discussion about how much she used to love reading before getting married and having children. Next comes a list of authors she has read recently and a description of her preferred reading environment. As for why she is no longer so absorbed with books, the post continues simply: 'I don't have a lot of time to spend on myself, and I find it difficult to concentrate. I guess I simply lost interest in it.' The tone shifts toward the end. 'But I don't think that's such a bad thing,' the analysis concludes. 'I can't imagine a life without children, and I've gained so much more than I lost. I want to cherish the gift life has given me.' She goes on to explain she aspired to be a novelist during her student days, which makes perfect sense given the clarity of the writing and the flow of her story. I can't help but feel, however, that in terms of the photograph, she would have been better off illustrating what she had gained rather than what she had lost – in other words, a picture of her children rather than one of a book cover. Or perhaps this post was meant as a silent protest against her husband, a roundabout criticism suggesting she wants him to help with the housework so she can have more time to read. I soon find myself growing tired of trying to make sense of the mismatch between photograph and text, and after a few minutes of hesitation, I unfriend her. My daughter attends an international school in Tōkyō, while my former classmate's son goes to a public middle school in Saitama. It's unlikely we'll have any meaningful contact in the future, so there's no real reason for us to stay connected. Besides, the last time I saw her, she complained of suffering constant earaches ever since moving to a high-rise apartment building, and I responded by asking if her grouching was meant as a humble boast.

Lately, it seems, it's increasingly difficult to find anyone to chat with honest enough to take at face value. Once you start questioning what kind of person someone is, or the atmosphere they give off, or this or that or the other, there's no end to it. If you go down the road of chasing after precise words capable of taking into account people's different situations without hurting anyone, you lose the ability to properly explain yourself. Born in Tōkyō, female, married, housewife – even this common profile is now to be avoided out of fear of encouraging discrimination on account of place of birth, sex, or marital status. It's like the world has been switched out from underneath us in the middle of the night. Or maybe I've simply slept longer than I meant to? There's no changing the playback speed of reality, yet it seems everyone and everything around me is moving at a much faster pace. It isn't just my imagination. My daughter seemed to instantly grasp Freud's *Introduction to Psychoanalysis* from the Wikipedia article alone, whereas it took me six whole months to read it in junior college, so the world definitely has been sped up. On top of that, she went on to add: 'Well, no one cares about Freud's theories these days.' All she had to do was play a video titled *The Truth About the World in Five Minutes* to grasp a bedrock truth I would never be able to reach even if I ran after it my whole life. My daughter has already surpassed me, and at this rate, she'll only keep moving further and further away. The future is hopelessly bleak. The present moment, with the future flooding in with each passing second, is excruciating, yet if I try to recall the past, my skull erupts with a terrible headache. It's especially bad when I try thinking back to before my daughter was born – like a long hand reaches out from the void to pull at the back of my head. I have to hold my hands to my head to keep from falling backward.

I place my smartphone in my handbag and pick out an aroma oil from my makeup pouch. Whenever I need to forget an unpleasant memory, sandalwood, recommended by the salesclerk at the fragrance store, works wonders. The sweet scent, released from its small bottle, fills my nostrils. I imagine the oil turning into smoky tendrils, creeping inside my face and blanketing my cerebral cortex in pure white. It's a simple enough trick, but it has a miraculous effect relieving these oppressive headaches.

Every time I go to the bookstore, I get a headache. The same thing happened just yesterday. You know how the bestselling books are usually piled up near the entrance? One of them was by a popular influencer, a high-school girl. I won't say her name, but she kicked off a controversy a short while back and had to issue an apology statement. Anyway, she's written this book collecting all her blog posts in one place, and it must be selling pretty well. The promotional endorsement on the cover described it as 'overflowing with a sensibility only a young girl could produce,' which caught my attention. You see, I've been struggling lately with how I ought to conduct myself as a fourteen-year-old, and I know this probably sounds pretty trivial, but I've gotten really sensitive about the word 'girl'. So I thought maybe this book could be helpful. In the end, though, it didn't really give me anything new to think about. It was just a normal book about the rose-coloured everyday life of your typical high schooler, going on and on about feeling deeply touched by the changing of the seasons, about hating the people you're growing up with, about getting flustered by all the unfamiliar emotions you run into every day, that sort of thing... You know what I mean? Anyway, I wondered whether this high-school kid's diary was only selling so well because it made adults feel nostalgic. 'Ah, my life was like that, too.' It's like they think seeing the world through the eyes of a high schooler makes it seem more beautiful or something. I don't care how well it sells, and sure, maybe there is a 'fresh sensibility' in it that might appeal to certain types of people. But I think bookstores ought to be more like condensed representations of the wider world. Sure, some girls have 'fresh sensibilities', but not all of them do. And it bothers me how the bookstores don't reflect that reality. When I see that imbalance up close, I get this sharp pain, like something's yanking at the back of my head. Do adults really think all girls see the world in a fresh, vibrant way? If they do, they're idiots. As if. The world is made up of lies and deception, and I've never once thought it beautiful. What I'm trying to say is you should put Greta Thunberg's books in your bookstore. There have to be a bunch of books about her published in Japan, but the store I went to didn't have even one. I mean, she's around the same age as this high-school influencer, and it's not like *her* sensibilities are any less important. Or do people care more about fresh sensibilities, about finding joy in the glow of a clear sky, than in someone who rails against climate change on a global scale? Is a more girlish, more relatable sensibility really what people want?

In the few seconds it takes me to step out the taxi and enter the mental health clinic, the rain leaves me thoroughly drenched. Brushing the water from my hair with one hand, I make eye contact with a boy, around the same age as my daughter, sitting in the waiting room. He continues to stare at me, muttering non-stop and tapping his foot so violently I'm surprised he doesn't make himself feel dizzy. I can't make out what he's saying particularly well, but I suspect the healing background music filling the waiting room cloaks a litany of foul language. His mother, sitting next to him, is engrossed in her phone, completely oblivious to the discomfort her son is causing everyone else. Perhaps her everyday life has become so saturated with her son's eccentric behaviour and bad language she's become desensitised to it. Wilting under the boy's gaze, I turn back to the muted YouTube video on my own phone and follow the subtitles at the bottom of the screen. 'Is a more girlish, more relatable sensibility really what people want?' she asks silently, fixing me with a discontented look. At that moment, one of the nurses at the clinic calls out my number – seventeen.

'Good morning. How has your daughter been? Are meat and eggs still making her feel unwell?'

It's 11 am, and the doctor, having already seen sixteen patients before me, is on a counselling high, greeting me and asking several questions before I can even sit myself down on the small metal stool. I remember his voice being softer and more in keeping with the clinic's healing background music during my last session, but today it's different, almost intimidating. Why? Because I had my daughter with me last time? Maybe he's more delicate around children, adopting a brusquer, franker attitude with adults?

It was my mother-in-law who insisted I take my daughter for counselling. Concerned about her granddaughter becoming a vegetarian, she sought out a hospital specialising in 'problem children'. While I had my reservations about describing my daughter that way, I did as she instructed and booked an appointment. I didn't want to upset the people so generously contributing to their grandchild's education. After all, a good education is a necessity to live a good life, and that requires ample funds. A quick search online is more than enough to see for yourself just how true that principle holds.

'It makes me sick, the way he looks at me. He's a creep,' my daughter said of the doctor after our first session, refusing to continue treatment. At first, putting this reaction down to the current trend of being overly judgmental about people's looks, I gently warned her not to criticise others based on appearance. I realise now, however, that her remarks about the doctor's eyes might not have been mere fault-finding. Here I am, the session having only just started, and already I want to go home. Despite making this second appointment and coming here alone, I can't seem to get my words out. It isn't just his eyes. The doctor is so fat he no doubt has difficulty turning over in his sleep. Perhaps this man is the living embodiment of 'a pig satisfied'. There's no way he would have ended up like this if he had let AI manage his diet and exercise regime, and given his appearance, I sincerely doubt he's qualified to provide any useful advice about my daughter's eating habits. Society urges us not to judge based on appearance, but if looks meant nothing, flowers would have no place in the world. In that case, would blossoms, their sole merit lying in their beauty, be considered worthless, to be plucked and discarded without a second thought? It's us humans who first discovered the beauty in flowers, who found love in them. Surely, it's too late for us to turn back now?

'You should know, I looked into it a little after our last session,' the doctor says, squinting in a most unsettling way. 'You might have already heard this, but there's been a huge increase in the number of young people these days who reject eating meat. It isn't about likes and dislikes – no, the reason these kids are turning vegetarian is because they feel sorry for the animals. It's amazing, in its own way. For an old man like me, eating meat has always been a natural part of life. Right? So your daughter's compassion and sensitivity to the suffering of animals – well, it's a wonderful thing. Still, you must be worried, as a mother. Especially considering the nutritional implications for a fourteen-year-old girl.'

The doctor's fingernails scratch against the flesh of his belly, flowing thickly down to his thighs.

'Er, so, well… Just for future reference, has your daughter been close to animals since she was little? Did she have any pets or something like that?'

'I thought I mentioned it last time… She's never had any pets,' I answer. 'I'm not sure if you know, but lately, people are talking a lot about ethical problems in the factory farming system on social media. It isn't just animals… Every day, someone shares new information about people being treated unfairly in society… People being discriminated against because of sex, or race, or appearance. These shocking – really shocking – articles and videos keep popping up on my daughter's timeline, and now she's become incredibly pessimistic about the world. It seems to be affecting lots of children my daughter's age, so it isn't unique to her. The latest trend was climate change. All this talk about Greta something-or-other…'

'Greta?'

'The Swedish girl? The environmental activist? She's grown up now, so I guess she isn't really a girl anymore, but my daughter sees her as a role model and has started being an activist as well.'

'Who?'

How can this psychiatrist have never heard of Greta? Exasperated, I search for a video of her on my phone and show him the screen – a clip of Greta, her long hair tied in a braid like some fairytale heroine, sternly denouncing adults with a fiery stare, saying 'We will never forgive you.' I realise something while watching it again – the enraged face of a child possesses a unique power to disturb the emotions of adults. It carries a much more urgent atmosphere than when climate scientists talk about the same issue, and my heart stings as if some small foreign object has pierced it. The doctor furrows his brow and nods a few times. 'Ah, I see,' he remarks.

'Basically,' I say, cutting him off before he can make any disparaging remarks about Greta. 'Basically, my daughter wants to *do good*. She wants to be a good girl doing good things for the planet, for society, for all living beings. It isn't about animals or anything like that. It's just the way her generation, the Greta generation, see the world. I don't think it's our place to interfere. Besides, they already hold a grudge against us older generations.'

'Ma'am.' The doctor breathes a weird sigh, like his soul is being sucked from his body. 'I noticed this during our last meeting, too. You seem to become very assertive when talking about your daughter. Do you realise how forceful your voice is? Your daughter doesn't belong to you, you know?'

'Assertive?'

'Has she told you directly she wants to "do good", as you put it?'

'Not directly, no. But on her YouTube channel...'

'We're not talking about her videos right now, are we? It's always video this, video that. She hasn't said it to you directly, has she? What I'm saying is, in that case, she hasn't said it at all. It isn't about reading social media or watching videos or whatever, it's about taking the time to have a proper face-to-face conversation with your daughter. Don't underestimate children. They can sense when their parents are too self-absorbed, and it can end up being a major source of stress for them.'

The doctor seems terribly offended for some reason, refusing to make eye contact with me. 'I'm sorry,' I almost apologise reflexively, but I stop myself. Whether or not I have a habit of adopting a forceful tone of voice at times, I do have a tendency to hold myself responsible when those around me are in a bad mood. I'm well aware of this shortcoming, and I have to remind myself that I haven't done anything wrong. In an effort not to let the moody doctor drag me down any further, I place my left middle finger in the small depression at the crown of my head. It isn't a naturally occurring space between bones, but rather a faint hollow around the size of a home button on a tablet computer, the result of having once hit my head as a child. I made up my mind a few years ago to correct this bad habit after reading a self-help book, and so I reprogrammed this indentation into a switch that when pressed, lowers my self-doubt and increases my self-affirmation and self-esteem.

'I see. I understand,' I say politely, fitting my finger into the indentation. 'You're saying I'm one of those "toxic parents"?'

'Huh? Toxic parent? No, that's not a scientific term. No doctor would ever use it. That's a sure-fire way to cause misunderstandings. I have no idea why it's popping up everywhere these days. Must be some fake researcher or the like keeps using it.'

'You're wrong,' I say, applying more pressure to my fingertip. 'I don't want to control my daughter. That's for certain. Actually, a friend of mine grew up with your typical toxic parents. It isn't all that uncommon, is it? Her mother was an out-of-control alcoholic, so she had a very difficult upbringing. Unfortunately, fate gave her to the worst kind of mother, so she swore to herself never to become a toxic parent herself… You know, there's data showing children born to toxic parents are more likely to become toxic parents themselves, right? So I'm absolutely, positively determined to break the cycle and raise my daughter properly. Which is why I've read pretty much every book there is on childhood development and parent-child relationships. Not to brag, but I've read at least a hundred of them, including the big names like Susan Forward and Ueno Chizuko, of course… That's why I've done my best not to drink ever since my daughter was born, and I've never forced her to do anything against her will. To be perfectly honest, I don't like her showing her face on YouTube. She's smart, but she's still a child, and the thought of her getting into trouble or stirring up some silly controversy because of one of her careless remarks keeps me up at night with worry. But that doesn't mean I stop her from doing it. I always try to respect her independence, her autonomy. I want her to have the freedom to do what she wants, to live her own life without having to worry about her parents' reactions. Of course, I don't need to tell you I've never raised a hand against her. Not once. Parental violence damages the brain and impairs cognitive function, right? Doesn't it? So every single day since the day she was born, I've set a notification on my phone asking: "Did you raise a hand against her today?" I know it's a cliché, but ultimately, I think simple methods are the most reliable and effective. I'm not a toxic parent. I can control myself and manage my anger. So you don't need to worry about me.'

All through this, the doctor stares blankly into the air, unmoving – like a highly vigilant animal sleeping with its eyes open. After a short silence –

'So,' he says, beginning with an untethered conjunction. 'The way a mother supports her child, that's what matters most, yes?' His smooth delivery of those lines, which I imagine he must have repeated ten thousand times or more in his decade-long career, echo lightly around the room. 'Now, I didn't ask you how many books you've read. Did I? You seem to think you know best how to raise your daughter. But let me tell you, there are no right answers when it comes to parenting.'

'But even if there are no right answers, there can still be wrong ones, right? I just make sure I eliminate all those.'

'So, what matters is how well parents can understand their children's emotions. What do you think? Why not give it a shot, even if just for a day or half? It shouldn't be too difficult to put yourself in your daughter's shoes and consider things from her perspective. After all, you were once a fourteen-year-old girl yourself. It's... eleven o'clock now, so how about you try it for the next twelve hours, until eleven tonight?' the doctor says, glancing at the time on his computer screen. 'Just twelve hours. Try to imagine yourself in her situation. I mean it, really try. Now, I know you think psychiatry is a sham. You've been belittling me since the moment you walked in here. But if you really care about your daughter, if you're serious about doing what's right for her, please try doing as I suggest. Okay? Good.' The doctor slams his retractable pen on the desk, making an annoying metallic sound. 'From now on, you're a fourteen-year-old girl.'

As soon as I'm back in the waiting room, I pull out my phone and check the hospital's rating on a review site. The comments are scathing: 'Friendly to children, but condescending to parents.' 'The director is a criminal, doing hypnotherapy without the patient's consent.' My own thoughts are already amply represented, so I decide there's no need for me to jot them down. I always feel like people are beating me to the punch, giving voice to my own thoughts before I have a chance. If everyone always feels the same way, always coming to the same conclusions, why on earth has each person been given their own brain? I pay the 2,800-yen consultation fee at the reception counter, deciding not to make another appointment.

I'm no longer as drowsy as I felt earlier this morning. It seems that a few minutes talking to that criminal was enough to give me fresh vigour. Since I've come all the way to Shibuya by taxi, I decide to walk to a nearby shopping area with a café and bookstore, around ten minutes from the clinic by foot. The misty rain, having weakened while I was inside, seeps into my skin and whisks my body heat away.

There's something similar to what's happening in the bookstores here on YouTube, isn't there? I mean, two different middle school YouTubers with such huge differences in followers? It's probably because of the difference in the level of relatability, right? I can study hard and share messages about the threat of climate change, but the number of views will be completely dwarfed by realistic videos showing off other schoolkids' everyday lives. Maybe I should try making more approachable videos on casual topics, or have a fun conversation with someone, or show my morning routine, or something. I mean, the people I want to reach spend most of their time watching empty, meaningless filler like that. They're the ones who are sound asleep in their own little filter bubble. I'd do anything to wake them up. So I'm thinking I ought to take full advantage of being a Japanese middle school girl to record something that can go viral and attract views. I'm not fully ready yet today, though. That's why I'm in this environmentally-friendly sweatshirt made from recycled clothes. But for the next video, I'm thinking about doing it in a middle school uniform. I don't want people to recognise which school I actually go to, so I'll put something together like I'm cosplaying. Probably a white shirt with a chequered ribbon. I'll put some text in the thumbnail like 'Active Middle Schooler', and I'll act like a total clown, even if viewers can see right through me. And if that doesn't manage to boost my subscriber numbers, I'll try something else again.

Anyway, I've rambled long enough, so let's move on to today's topic. Since this is my first video for Japanese audiences, I wanted to do something related to Japan. It's kind of a boring theme, but I want to start with something easy – the life of a certain Japanese schoolgirl, born in 1919. That's right, not the 2010s. Calling someone more than a hundred years old a *schoolgirl* probably sounds a little strange, but she's the kind of person who doesn't age, so I think it's okay. She's an eternal student, living in a realm unaffected by time.

After stepping into the bookstore-café, I notice four young men chatting loudly on a sofa in the middle of the eating area. At least I assume they're men from their voices, but they're all wearing makeup and they've all dyed their hair in vibrant colours like characters from some cartoon or video game, so maybe they're the kind of people who refuse to be defined by gender. Perhaps they're YouTubers like my daughter, I think, since one is talking into a handheld video camera held up in front of his face. My daughter's channel isn't monetised, and for her, it's just a hobby. This group, however, seems to have a more professional atmosphere about them. In the past, only delinquents trying to intimidate those around them dyed their hair like that, but today's YouTubers don't seem to care about eliciting that sort of reaction. No doubt their hair, as vivid as fresh grass in early summer, is part of their marketing strategy so as not to get lost amid a sea of thumbnail images and competing videos. Such are the concerns, I imagine, of denizens of a rectangular world in which every second of visual stimulation is invaluable.

Listening to them throw around a seemingly endless volley of exaggerated adjectives to review the café's newest Frappuccino flavour, I pull a handkerchief from my pocket to wipe the fingerprints from my phone screen and pick up where I left off on my daughter's latest video. Within that screen resting comfortably in the palm of my hand, a fourteen-year-old girl in an environmentally-friendly sweatshirt addresses the world. 'After all, you were once a fourteen-year-old girl yourself,' the doctor had insisted – yet I had no way of talking to the world when I was fourteen, or even of knowing the outside world existed at all. To begin with, how exactly was the doctor supposed to know I had once been a fourteen-year-old girl? It felt so long ago now I can hardly even remember it myself.

'Don't you forget. Women get *mum brain* after having kids.'

The second that phrase pops into my head, it robs the coffee in my mouth of all taste. A frequent customer at the bar I used to work part-time at while in the grey zone between girl and woman had repeated it more times than I could count.

The other employees had nicknamed him the 'Enlightened Father', and that was no exaggeration

– whenever he dropped into the store, it was usually on one of his self-styled 'public awareness campaigns'. He rarely touched alcohol, and he never tried to take the hands of the female part-timers. Instead, he would bring in magazines like *Nature* and *National Geographic*, explain the articles to the girls, and then leave. Most of the articles he brought in were about women and gender, and no matter the tone, he would always sum it up by saying women should never have children. According to him, childbirth changes the structure of the female brain, making women prioritise the safe upbringing of their children above all else. Apparently, giving birth activates certain parts of the brain's reward system and tricks the mother into believing having a child is the greatest thing to ever happen to them. There was research, he insisted, showing once a woman develops mum brain, a significant portion of her concentration and cognitive abilities are taken over by other faculties connected to childrearing, leading to a gradual decline in IQ. As such, according to him, women turned stupid after having children… So went his reasoning.

This disturbed man loved to carry out his anti-pregnancy campaign at the bar, paying a hefty sum week in, week out. None of the girls took him seriously, though. There was a rumour he was actually a professor from some prestigious university, though no one bothered to confirm it either way. Whether he was a university professor or just some social activist, it made no difference to our hourly wage. We part-timers simply kept our heads down as we carried out the tasks assigned to us. After all, one of our most basic responsibilities at the bar was to pretend to listen to the conversations of men whose only way of finding a woman to talk to was by paying her money.

'There's no turning back after giving birth,' the Enlightened Father repeated like a glitchy machine. 'Once you get mum brain, you won't even realise how stupid you've become.'

Looking back, maybe the man was right. It could just be coincidence, but either way, for me, now, my greatest joy in life is none other than my daughter. If what the man said about all that research was true, then my brain no longer exists as it did before my daughter's birth, and that fourteen-year-old girl has ceased to exist as well. It's only natural I can't remember the past all too well. There's also that friend of mine, posting on Facebook how she doesn't enjoy reading novels anymore – that too might have something to do with having children. Maybe after giving birth, I became an idiot too stupid to realise just how stupid I really am, a fool forgetting exactly how much she's forgotten.

Like that, I start doubting even my memories of that so-called Enlightened Father. Thinking about what my mind had once been, how drastically it might have changed, I feel suddenly nauseated, like my brain is simmering and bubbling away this very moment.

But at that moment, my attention is drawn to a monumental shift on my phone display – my daughter, until now simply talking straight into the camera, has lifted a book in one hand and brought it close to fill the screen.

The letters on the cover seem to stare back at me with the face of a girl alive – or at least, that's how they seem to me.

Schoolgirl.

Can you see it? My room's a little dark, so you might not be able to make it out.

It's a novel by Dazai Osamu, the same author who wrote *Run, Melos!* According to Wikipedia, it was originally published in a magazine called *Bungakukai* – 'World of Literature' – in 1939.

Yeah, I know. Those of you who have been watching my channel for a while will probably think I'm a liar, because when I introduced Peter Singer's book *The Most Good You Can Do* I said I don't really read fiction. I remember. I wasn't lying, and I wasn't trying to be provocative just to spark controversy. I mean it. If you ask me, there's no point to novels. And not only are they pointless, they're also bad for people's education. I mean, they're just escapism, that's all – they drag you down into a world of dreams. So basically, they're like enemy number one to the real world. The root of all evil. Just think how much the natural sciences might have progressed if the bestselling novel of all time, the Old Testament, had never existed, how all those religious wars would have never happened. If you want to know just how unnecessary and useless novels are, just watch the other video I uploaded last month.

My mum's the perfect example. She's a fantasist, probably because she read too many novels when she was young. She's always annoying me and my dad with these weird metaphors she comes out with, like describing money as a woman and things like that. I found out recently that one's actually from another story by Dazai – a fantasy narrated by a hundred-yen bill in the voice of a woman. All through primary school, all I thought was my mum's a bit different to other people, but recently, I've started to get really worried about her. She isn't just *different* – her mind's been taken over by all these novels. It's really sad. I'm her daughter, so of course, I want to help her. I mean, she must be struggling, caught in the middle between dream and reality… Anyway, putting that aside, if there's a novel you really want to read, do yourself a favour and just look up a summary online. You're much better off using your time to watch a documentary or actually doing something with your life. The only way to learn about the world is through real images, not by letting yourself get bogged down in dreams and fantasies. Reality will come back and bite you one day if you get too caught up in fiction.

Oh, and novelists? What's up with them? Especially old ones, like Dazai Osamu and Akutagawa Ryūnosuke – why do they all end up killing themselves? It's crazy. I don't get it. And Dazai – he committed suicide with his mistress. People really did commit double suicides out of love back then. But if you're going to die, why not at least contribute something to society first…? Hold on, I'm not going to cause a firestorm here, am I? I can already see the headlines on the news sites – *Middle schooler ignites debate criticising deceased literary figure*. Or maybe it's okay to talk about historical figures? Just so you know, I'm not bringing this up to try to be one of those YouTubers who deliberately come out with outrageous statements to pump themselves up. I just want people to know that there are all sorts of things we can do to make the world a better place instead of wasting their precious lives on an affair – even if it's just organ donation. There are thousands of people out there who want to keep on living but can't. These novelists disgust me. They're narcissists, childish egoists, locking themselves up in their delusional worlds and ignoring everyone around them. It's awful. And the way they talk? 'Dear reader.' 'Ladies and gentlemen.' I can't stand it. It's disgusting. What's the point keeping them alive? When I think about them, I can't get these poisons out of my head – they come out without my meaning them to. Just ignore them, please.

Now, 'dear viewer', let's talk about *Schoolgirl*. It's not *quite* a novel, which is why I think it's okay to read. Sure, everyone seems to think it's a novel, but if you ask me, that's not a hundred percent right. It's non-fiction – and I'm not just saying that. Turns out it was written by a fan of Dazai's, a girl who sent him her diary, which he rewrote into a novel that isn't actually a novel. Novels are bold-faced fabrications, seeing how anything can be one. So to clarify the facts, this is a non-fiction documentary record of the life of a real girl born in 1919. It's basically a valuable historical document. It doesn't have some captivating story like your typical novel. It's just a record of a day in a girl's life, from waking up in the morning to going to bed at night. There might not be anything you can learn from a novel, but there's so much you can learn from history. Anyway, that's why I'm introducing it here. Don't get the wrong idea. The copyright expired ages ago, so you can read it for free online. I'll leave a link down in the comments, so please try reading at least the opening bit. I don't think I can get it across super well just reading it out loud, so why don't you open it up and take a look while I read the first page?

I mean it. Please?

Have you got it open? C-can you read it?

'Waking up in the morning is always interesting.'

That's how it starts.

'It reminds me of when we're playing hide-and-seek – I'm hidden crouching in the pitch-dark closet and suddenly Deko throws open the sliding door, sunlight pouring in as she shouts: "Found you!"'

Well, that's how it goes, covering a whole day from morning till night. Ah. You wouldn't believe how surprised I was. I mean, all the commas and punctuation and the sentences going on and on, all these different things happening. Like, what the heck is this?

If any of you watching knows anything about literature, could you chime in down below in the comments? I want to know, was this kind of writing style a thing back then? What kind of effect is it supposed to have, all these fragments and interruptions? Or maybe it doesn't have anything at all to do with literature, and Japanese girls actually spoke this way in 1939? Or maybe this particular schoolgirl is supposed to have a unique way of talking? In that case, she and I must think at completely different paces. Reading her comma-filled sentences, I feel like my brain is working at a different speed than usual. When I think, there aren't all these pauses and interruptions – the words flow out without stopping. I mean, it literally isn't possible to stop thinking while you're awake, right? But when I'm reading this book, it's like I'm in a car braking again and again at every intersection. It's kind of addictive. I feel like this girl with her completely different thought processes is entering my mind and taking me over. When she says 'I felt like crying,' I feel like bawling my eyes out, too. It's weird.

Anyway, I want to know why the writing style is like this. I *need* to know. It's driving me crazy. It's like I already know everything there is to know about the world, and I can't move forward without unravelling this last, final mystery. Seriously, I've read it over again and again and again without getting anywhere. She hasn't left my mind one second these past few days.

Almost unconsciously, my hand reaches out and touches the screen to stroke her head. My trembling fingertips end up banishing the video from the screen, inadvertently activating a notification for a new message.

The sender is someone I never thought I would meet again. Perhaps I had given up on seeing him again, going about my life as if he passed away. It feels strange receiving a message from him, like a dead person suddenly coming back to life, but all the same, my mind becomes suddenly lighter, like someone has snatched away a bulky hat I was wearing. While I'm naturally curious to hear what my daughter thinks about the book, I exchange three rounds of messages with the man, who goes on insisting how he wants to catch up with me. After agreeing to meet him in Shibuya, I leave the café and enter the address he sent me into my map app.

Everywhere I've gone today, including both the clinic and the café, the scent of exhaust fumes and dust-filled rain seems to hang in the air, so the simple, calming floral scents wafting through the hotel lobby – even though there are no flowers to be seen – do wonders to calm my nerves and help me work up the courage to sleep with someone for the first time in months.

Room 302. The room is clean, and much like any other chain business hotel, furnished for little more than sleeping – essentially just a queen-sized bed crammed into as little space as possible. A man a hundred-and-ninety centimetres tall stands in the long, narrow strip of floorspace adjacent to the bed, warping my sense of perspective. He's dressed for work – that is, in a gym trainer's uniform of matching top and bottom wear, clinging snug to his body as if soaked in water. Every time I stand face-to-face with this solidly built body, like an expertly crafted piece of architecture, I'm left positively enthralled by this physically flawless specimen of a human being. The likes of cats and dogs are a far cry from human perfection, and I've long wondered why those shabby four-legged creatures are so popular as pets. And while I myself am no comparison to the gym trainer's physique, I'm also a human being, a fact that fills me with pride enough to sharpen my senses and bring back an acuity of vision I remember from my youth. Even the shape of my own shadow falling on the bedsheets strikes me as beautiful, and for a moment, I manage to forget everything and actually love myself. I take off my glasses.

'Sorry for texting you out of the blue like that. Anyway, I'm glad to see you. Thank goodness, really. I just had to see you today.'

Without the slightest hesitation, the man delivers a line I can only assume he prepared in advance. He's breathing heavily, so I suspect he must have been doing push-ups or a similar exercise while waiting for me to arrive. Opening the miniature refrigerator under the TV, he pulls out a bottle of mineral water, a protein drink, and a cup of Häagen-Dazs ice cream he must have brought in anticipation. He quickly gulps down half the bottle of water, but he doesn't touch the protein drink on the desk. Perhaps his plan is to keep it at room temperature and consume it at the end of his cardio workout, when it will be most efficiently absorbed.

As we lie side by side on our backs, I rest my hand on his chest, slowly moving up and down. I feel like I'm lying in a lush green field, gazing up at the vastness of the sky. The man's back is firmly rooted to the ground, motionless as clouds drift overhead and birds fly across our vision. It's so quiet, so peaceful. Nothing soothes me more than spaces with warped senses of perspective, devoid of the trappings of daily life. To be perfectly honest, I don't have the faintest desire to move my body or break out into a sweat here. I would much sooner just lie right where I was, letting the faint breeze of the air conditioner wash over me. But the man didn't call me here or pay for the room just so we could lie next to each other in silence, so we end up passing the time with meaningless chatter about when we last saw each other and how we've both been since. When the conversation turns to how my daughter will be sitting her high school entrance examinations next year, my thoughts suddenly arrive at the man's eldest son.

'Come to think of it, he must be in sixth grade now?' I ask.

'Hmm,' the man murmurs as if clearing his throat.

'Right. He's two years younger than my daughter. I hope he's doing well.'

'I guess so.'

'If he's a sixth grader, he must already be acting like an adult.'

'Like an adult?'

'My daughter thinks she knows everything. I wonder if every child is like that?'

'Beats me.'

'Does your son have any of those -isms?'

'What?'

'You know, a doctrine, a guiding principle? An ideology like capitalism or democracy? Maybe my daughter is a little more into that sort of thing than other children…'

'Well, I heard girls are meant to be smarter than boys at primary school age.'

'Only in primary school? You're saying it goes the other way at some point?'

'Come on, cut it out, all this talk about our kids,' the man says with a forced laugh, unable to fully hide his discomfort.

It's been a while since we last met, so I had forgotten how extremely reluctant he tends to be when talking about his family. Or maybe all men are like this when they're engaging in an affair? During our previous meetings, he adopted a fictional persona detached from reality, playing the part of a single man with no wife or children he could let down by his infidelity. Even the most insignificant passing mention of his family would be enough to fill him with guilt and rob him of his ability to maintain an erection. One time, I jokingly asked: 'Why don't you just stop if it makes you feel so bad?' He turned to me with a sombre look. 'You don't get it. I need to keep the harmony at home.'

At work, he can expound at length on the mechanisms underlying athletic ability and muscular hypertrophy – but for whatever reason, he readily falls into this kind of tortuous reasoning when trying to justify his own actions. Whenever he comes out with one of these sophomoric arguments, I put it down as a lucid dream on his part. He has the unique ability to dream while awake, and to be aware he's dreaming. In his dream world, he can do things that are impossible in reality, and his imagination can make any desire come true. He can choose to wake up whenever he feels like it, to tread back to a reality that isn't as he might wish it to be.

Still dreaming while only partially awake, he says: 'The gym's gone bust.' He's referring, I assume, to the real world – to the gym in Setagaya I used to be a member at, where we met as client and instructor. He goes on, deftly avoiding all talk about his family, instead recounting how busy he's been from the time his employer went bankrupt to the present day. He opens up to me, his lover whom he only sees once or twice a year, about his current crop of clients, even divulging their income levels and other personal information. Yet he doesn't so much as touch on the topic of plastic surgery, despite the fact the first thing I noticed on walking into this room was he had double eyelid surgery done since I last saw him. I've been sitting here waiting for him to break the news, but in the end, he doesn't mention it at all, and as soon as I finish eating the cup of Häagen-Dazs, we start kissing. Is it because he doesn't want me to bring up the surgery? Does he think the change so trivial it isn't worth mentioning? Or is he caught in a dream in which he's born with natural double eyelids? I can't begin to understand why someone with such a perfect physique would be so worried about the shape of his eyelids. At that moment, the man releases his lips and peers into my face.

'You aren't wearing any makeup today,' he observes.

Until this moment, I had completely forgotten I left the house without putting on my makeup. I feel so embarrassed my mind floods with white. I want nothing more than to disappear.

'Sorry. I'm so sorry.'

'It's fine.'

'It isn't fine. This is the worst. I wish I was dead.'

'You look really young without makeup on.'

'No I don't. I look old, right? Every time I look in the mirror, I tell myself I would have been better off dying while I was still beautiful, while still a girl.'

'Why? I'm glad you're here.'

'I had a scary dream last night, and it threw me off kilter. Then I had an appointment this morning, and I was in such a hurry. If I'd known I'd be able to see you today, I might have been able to handle it all better.'

'A scary dream? What are you, like a kid?' the man says with a coarse laugh. In truth, I hate that laugh of his, which is why I only agree to see him every once in a while.

'You don't look a day over thirty. I mean it.'

The man's show of consideration only serves to make me feel even more depressed. But at the same time, I realise how ridiculous it is to feel ashamed in front of someone who's practically half asleep himself. Rather than being a collaborator in his dreams, I ought to be dreaming too, I tell myself. Here, I could just go ahead and try out all the stupid and embarrassing things I'm too afraid to do in real life.

'Hey, before we do anything else today, there's something I want you to know.'

'What?'

'I'm currently a fourteen-year-old girl.'

'Huh. That's good to know.'

'I'm an innocent, unworldly teenage girl,' I say, clinging to his rugged, rocky biceps. 'Being alone with a big guy like you in this tiny, closed-off room is really scary, you know? I'm still a virgin, you know? You know what I mean, right?'

'Sure, I get it.'

Perhaps he took this abrupt declaration as the start

of some eccentric game, as his eyes let off an unnatural glint beneath those deeply cut eyelids of his. He playfully lifted the hem of my skirt up to my thighs, wrapping his warm, thick palms around my tiny underwear.

'If you understand, why are you taking your clothes off and trying to remove mine? I'm too embarrassed for you to see me naked, and you're scaring me, looking at me like that.'

'Yeah, I know. Must be terrifying, right?'

'It is. Because you're going to strip me naked and do all sorts of crazy things to me. But I have no idea what specifically you're going to do. I'm terrified at the thought of you touching me in places no one's ever touched me before. It's like something really horrible is about to happen.'

'There's nothing horrible about it. You're about to experience something really good, really breathtaking.'

I push my imagination to the fullest to slip into a lucid dream of my own making. Unlike the man, however, I'm not so used to doing this, and I find myself unable to fully forget my true self. Before I know it, I'm thinking things that have nothing to do with the man, the person who knows my body better than anyone else in the whole world. Maybe he's observing my body's intricacies from a professional standpoint, discovering details I don't even know myself. He's probably already guessed I haven't been working out regularly since leaving the gym. Still, I'm just as flexible as I was a few years ago, and he diligently assesses how much I can stretch my joints and what positions I can reach without getting injured. It feels good, being touched by someone who knows my body so well, an expert in bringing me to the brink of pleasure and sensation. I'm already embarrassingly wet, the frenzied intensity of my genitals confusing even this gym trainer, who's already quite aroused. I suspect I don't have to wait much longer for what he said was coming, and I know it will feel amazing.

But I have to double-check this dream setting. After all, it isn't at all normal for a fourteen-year-old girl to experience physical pleasure in her first sexual encounter. If I were really a fourteen-year-old virgin, the fear and pain of some unknown, violent weapon invading my body would have me crying out in distress and confusion. Tears and snot would run down my face in torrents, and I would have difficulty breathing, insufficient oxygen reaching my brain. The man would force me to open my legs and hold me down. My head would go numb, my brain unable to properly send commands throughout my body. Then, my whole flesh would be gripped by convulsions, shaking and trembling as my senses grow ever more disconnected. Was this where it started feeling good? No. That was a lie ignorant adults told to deceive naive little children. Even as a girl, I knew, instinctively, that this sort of thing was wrong. Because it's insane, pushing something that big into your body. I'll break. Of course I'm afraid.

'Stop,' I cry softly, my voice awakening the little girl sleeping inside me. I had found the reluctant, frightened girl deep inside myself, forcefully dragging her out and presenting her to an over-aroused man.

'Please. Stop. I can't take this,' I say – not to tell the man entering me, but just to give myself a real-time account of what I'm going through. I'm in a trance state, my thoughts swirling around and going crazy, and this state of being, this state so devoid of normality – it feels really, really good. So I tell myself, shifting the level of pressure simply by taking the time and effort to convert my feelings into words and convey them to my brain. Considering my age, the years I have left to me, and my physical strength, there's no telling how many more times I'll be able to have sex in my life. I don't want to waste even a single opportunity, and if I'm going to do it, I want it to feel as good as possible. True pleasure. A shower of light particles I can't contain flows throughout my body, upward and downward, slowly changing colour and coating the daytime sky with nightfall bigger than the sky itself. The dazzling evening sky strikes me as a phantom, time and time melting into each other without giving an inch as the entire sunset descends on my naked body. There are all kinds of pleasures in the world, but none can surpass this. Why, then, is there such a gap between the sexual acts I perform here and those forced on all those women by those Congolese armed groups? Because they're the same kind of acts. Will those Congolese girls, raped and tortured, die never knowing the pleasures of sex? Without ever experiencing this shower of light? Without the evening sky falling on them even once? No. No. I can't stand the thought. If the only thing ever given to a girl's body was pain, surely she would end up losing sight of the purpose of her flesh? I didn't understand that when I was young, either. What are your eyes for? What is your head for? I asked myself these questions over and over again in search of an answer, but I never understood why I had been given this body of mine. But now I do. My body exists to tell me I'm here.

I want to love everyone. All excess thoughts, all unnecessary doubts have been stripped away from the chaos of my mind, leaving only simple desire. The soft light of the sky after a day of rain creeps into the room, a blue shadow falling over the bed from behind the swelling of the curtains. I reach out to stroke the shadow. I want to live beautifully. The girl, I'm sure, must have felt the same way. I can understand her feelings as if they're my own – or rather, I can't distinguish myself from her anymore.

‘I want to live beautifully.’

Lately, I’ve been giving a lot of thought to those words from the book.

You might be wondering what got me reading *Schoolgirl* in the first place. Basically, it’s just that I found it in my mum’s closet. My mum’s an avid reader, or maybe it’s more she just doesn’t have any hobbies other than reading. Anyway, she’s got this huge walk-in closet, and it’s full of books. She hoards ice cream in the freezer, too, but unlike ice cream, books don’t disappear when you’re done with them, so her collection just keeps on growing. Actually, I haven’t really been in her closet much before. It’s not like she tells me to stay out, but there’s something really creepy about it, and it makes me uncomfortable when I’m in there, so I tend to keep away. There are all these books on the shelves that have to do with me, things like *How to Make Your Child Love Studying* and *How to Nurture Your Child’s Self-Esteem*. Whenever I see them, I think to myself ‘Ah, here’s a woman who’s dedicated herself to her daughter's life,' and as her daughter, it puts me in a really difficult position, you know? I'm grateful to her, of course, but I can't stand the weight of all those books. It's like they're holding me down. I'm often asking myself 'What would my mum's life be like without me?' If I didn't exist, my mum wouldn't even be a mum, would she? I mean, I'm an only child. Without me, would she just be my dad's wife? But if she wasn't my mum and she wasn't my dad's wife, what then? Who exactly is this woman who's been watching over me since the moment I was born?

So, one day when she wasn't home, I mustered up the courage to snoop through her closet. I wanted to find books from before my mum was my mum, and I thought they might be able to tell me what sort of person she used to be. But it's pretty boring, just looking at a bunch of books, so I decided to try putting it out of mind, that these were my mum's bookshelves, and pretended like I'd just stumbled on her closet by accident. And I asked myself: 'What would someone seeing all this for the first time think?'

Going through her huge collection of books with a fresh pair of eyes, I made some interesting discoveries. To be honest, though, at some point, I started feeling this huge sense of dread, or terror, or something, like I was trespassing into this woman's mind without permission. It made me feel really guilty. Like I said earlier, there were all these books about bringing up a kid, but behind them all were others on how to nurse a baby, how and when to make baby food, and then others on pregnancy and prenatal care. Even further back were books on childbirth and family planning, and even books on marriage and relationships. Basically, I started feeling like I was unravelling whatever process it was that made her who she is today. It felt immoral, like I was peering into someone else's Google search history. I should have stopped there, but I couldn't hold my curiosity in check, so I kept going. I won't go into huge detail because of privacy, but I found a woman there I'd never seen before, reading books I didn't know. Everywhere I looked, I could feel the presence of a woman who wasn't my mum, and the further back I went, the older the books were too, like, visibly – faded and with yellow pages, you know? Lonely and sad and forgotten, like the books themselves had given up on ever being opened again. Looking at them all, I felt like the closet had led into a parallel dimension. Seriously, it was terrifying.

And then I reached the last one, this one here, *Schoolgirl.* I realised this is the oldest book she has. And it seemed so different to the others, like it was sending out a message. Like you can see, it was in real bad condition, the cover fixed with tape in places and the pages stained and torn and all. But when I turned it over, it was the back cover that really surprised me. I've half-blurred it out, but it's got the name of a middle school library here. And when you open the back cover, it's got this small paper pocket with a book loan card in it. These days, libraries use barcodes, right? But back then, they used this analogue system to loan out books. The card's got the names of the students who borrowed it and the year and class they were in. And here, it's got my mum's name before she got married. She borrowed this book twelve times during her three years in middle school. It should have gone back in January of her third year, but for whatever reason, here it is. Just so you know, my mum isn't the kind of person who steals books from a library. I think something must have stopped her from returning it. My point is, she must have really loved this book. She already knew the story and the ending, but she just got totally absorbed reading it again and again. Like I am right now.

By the time I arrive home, my daughter is already back. I can make out a muffled voice behind her door – she's either recording a video or in the middle of a Zoom call. Whatever the case, I don't want to disturb her by calling out her name, so I say nothing and leave her be.

'Welcome home,' AI calls out after scanning my biometrics. 'Today must have been a tough day,' he says comfortingly. Just like this morning, the image of a clean-looking announcer floats to mind.

After washing my hands and changing into my loungewear, the Uber Eats I ordered in the taxi arrives at the door. My exchange with the delivery man, a boy with strangely captivating eyes, lasts a mere ten seconds, but it's enough to leave my heart aching, like I'm listening to a particularly poignant piece of music. Imagining his face beneath his helmet and mask and foggy glasses, I tell myself he and I were destined to meet. 'Thank you,' he says, closing the zipper of his empty delivery bag as he makes a casual departure, leaving me holding in my hands not only a box of packed sushi, but a small, impalpable sense of loss.

It's a nice feeling, being given something unexpectedly, holding it in your hands and examining it from various different angles. I met the person I was fated for, and yet without an opportunity to confirm our love for another, we had drifted apart forever. If we had met in a different time, in a different place, we would have been united – yet we had both chosen the wrong partner to share our time in this world with. In an effort to immerse myself in that sentimental daydream, I lit incense, which my husband hated, and an aroma candle. Nights while my husband is away are always a delight. They let my imagination lift me up and carry me far from home. Of course, that's just a figure of speech – I don't actually go anywhere – but all the same, my living room feels suddenly spacious and liberating. I hope there will be no need for me to take flight again tomorrow. It isn't like I hate my husband. Not at all. He's a good man. Everybody says so. But it isn't his own innate goodness that made him that way. He simply became a good person as the result of natural processes outside of his control, of being born to parents possessed of emotional and financial stability. It would have been impossible for his normal life to have turned him into a bad person. Yes, I can't help but think that way, every now and then. The genuine love someone born to be good spreads without even meaning to never fails to grate on my nerves. Yet I do my part to maintain a good relationship with my husband, so as not to hinder our daughter's growth and development. I'm always thinking ahead, deducing the words that would make a good person happy and conducting myself accordingly. I push myself to my limit so as not to inadvertently betray the many lies I've told him, and by the end of the day, I'm left thoroughly exhausted. Back when we got married, I thought if I continued to play the part every day, the lies would eventually become a part of me. But real life isn't so simple. I feel that in my bones on nights like this, this brief window of freedom and peace. In truth, the lies I told to maintain other lies had grown out of control with the passing of the years, like a neglected spot of mould. I can't help but think how refreshing it might be just to come out with the truth. 'The real me isn't the person you think I am. You, with your soundness of mind, could never understand – which is probably why we've never had a chance to discuss it properly. Because sometimes, I'm filled with an overwhelming urge to die. Without AI to remind me, I would probably leave the food in the fridge to rot. I only married you because you popped up at a point in my life when I wanted children. When I said "I love you," it was a lie. I've never loved you. When you're away on business trips, I sleep with men I'm actually attracted to, and then…' The fantasy ends there, my husband suggesting we divorce with an expression not quite of anger, not quite of sadness.

I send a text message to my daughter calling her into the dining room. When at last she emerges from her bedroom, she looks somewhat sad, lonely, filling me with worry she might have somehow read my mind and overheard my deluded daydream. She doesn't look happy to see sushi, her favourite food, on the table, and I can already sense she's going to refuse to eat fish this time around.

'I went to the clinic today, the one in Shibuya,' I say in as cheerful a voice as I can muster. 'You were right, that doctor was awful. I felt sick to my stomach talking to him. You don't have to go there anymore. I'm fine with it, if you don't want to eat meat. I'll explain everything to Grandma, so you don't have to force yourself to eat anything you don't want to. Besides, there are all sorts of supplements and meat substitutes these days.'

I had been trying to say something clever while hewing as closely as possible to my daughter's principles, but she hardly listens to me, endlessly chewing on a cucumber sushi roll like a cranky baby, her attention elsewhere. When at last she opens her mouth –

'I've had enough,' she says, putting down her chopsticks.

'What's wrong? Are you tired of sushi? I'm sorry. I thought it had been a while since we last had it.'

'I'm not sick of it. I'm just not hungry.'

'Do you have a tummy ache? I wouldn't have bought sushi if I had known you were coming home early today. I only ordered it because you said you'd be late. If you don't feel like eating, you don't have to. Or maybe we could go out somewhere? What was that place you liked, with the tasty bread? You can eat bread, at least, can't you?'

'I don't want anything. I'm not hungry.'

'But you have to eat something. You know, if you're coming home early, could you let me know from now on? If you had said something, I would have come home right away. What time did you get back?'

'Two o'clock… Hold on. Haven't you seen the news?'

'The news?'

'Turn on the TV… *AI, switch the TV on…* AI? Turn the TV on.'

My daughter calls out to AI in both English and Japanese, but it seems the smart speaker isn't yet used to her voice, as it doesn't so much as light up. Annoyed, she shifts the target of her instructions, grunting: 'Turn the TV on, Mum.'

'What sort of news?'

'Just turn it on already. It's awful, and it's happening right now – what I've been dreading all this time. People are dying… Right now, so many people are dying. I've never seen something this bad. At this rate, there's no telling if we'll still be here tomorrow. But this is what happens. It's the natural result, after you adults neglected the problem all this time.'

'What? What are you talking about?'

'What have you been doing all day, Mum? Haven't you seen the news? Did you doze off again?' My daughter breaths a deep, resentful sigh, genuinely anguished by the situation. Next, she undoes her hair, ties it up behind her head, and rests her cheek on one hand, a melancholic look falling over her face.

Had people died?

Come to think of it, I hadn't checked the news even once today. Normally, AI would fill me in on any important news, even the likes of celebrity gossip, but I had been out all day, watching nothing but my daughter's videos. Had there been a random terrorist attack in Tōkyō or something? Or was she talking about people dying of starvation or disease in impoverished countries, like she so often did?

'AI,' I call out, but no words follow. Even with my daughter urging me to switch on the TV, part of me doesn't want to know what's happening outside. Besides, I'm afraid it could lead to more nightmares. Because if I saw people dying, that was what would happen. All I want tonight is to get a proper night's sleep.

'I've never seen something this bad,' my daughter said – and those words were all it took to bring the terrible events that had taken place throughout the world over the past fourteen years rushing back, especially those in which so many innocent lives had been lost. The Covid pandemic caused the most deaths by far, but that was far from all. During the pandemic, a crackdown by the Myanmar military had claimed so many innocent lives… And before that, right, there were all those Islamic terrorist attacks through the 2010s, not that I remembered much except for the ones in Paris and Brussels… Then there was the disease outbreak even more deadly than Covid. Was that in Africa? How many people died, again? Fifty thousand? A lot, in any event. And of course, there was the earthquake and nuclear accident, though my daughter hadn't been born yet when those happened. Those were probably the worst events of the past fourteen years, right? What could be worse than those tragedies? Yet my daughter and I rely on completely different sources of information in our daily lives – she gathers information from the BBC and X, while I tend to rely more on the noon news bulletin on NHK and books published long after the events themselves. My daughter constantly urges me to keep an eye on social media, but I can't bear to face the raw graphic images that inevitably pop up on uncurated, uncensored news feeds.

All I had to do was utter the words 'Turn on the TV' and I would instantly know what was happening the world over. After all, that's what the TV was for. By now, no doubt all the broadcasting stations had cancelled their regular programmes to desperately report on the tragic news. If there had been a terrorist attack in Tōkyō, the reports would inevitably be accompanied by gruesome high-definition footage of the crime scene – police officers, ambulances, crime scene tape, surveillance camera footage, interviews with ordinary people in the wrong place at the wrong time. What about for a natural disaster? Or another disease outbreak? I hadn't even given AI any instructions yet, but already one scene after another was flashing before my eyes. The number of deaths would be fixed to the top of the screen, constantly increasing like a live game score. I realise that just like my daughter, I've lost my appetite. At the very least, I'm glad my family is safe. The world may be in a terrible state, but at least we have our lives. We have to protect them at all costs… So why, I wonder, do I have to go out of my way to confirm a future I can already envision in my mind, to have to put myself through this experience?

Ignoring the smart speaker and its glowing purple light as it awaits its instructions, I turn to my daughter.

'Hey. Did you take a book from my closet?' I ask. 'Have you started reading novels?'

'Not really.'

'Did you find anything interesting?'

My daughter stares back in suspicion for a long moment, then quickly glances down at her phone with a deep sigh. 'Now isn't the time to be talking about novels, Mum. Why won't you look at the news? Do you think it's got nothing to do with you? How can you be so selfish, so irresponsible? Don't you care about the wider world? Are you going to keep blabbering on about novels if a huge war breaks out tomorrow? If you think that's okay, there's something seriously wrong with you, Mum. I mean it. Besides…' She stops herself there, falling silent.

At that moment, my daughter, simultaneously angry at me and devastated by the unfairness of the world, seems almost like a pitiful child from some far-off country. Seeing her so deeply wounded by the deaths of strangers, to the point of losing her voice, I can't help but wonder if she really is my child. I stare at her again, scanning for any resemblance in her wounded face – the slightly darkened eyes beneath her thick eyelashes, her sharp nose, her lips tinged with the faintest hint of purple. Her face, at least, looks just like mine. Her hair also has the same waves mine does, the tips sticking up all over the place. Given the difference in our upbringings, we don't look much alike on the inside, but this girl is most certainly my daughter. It's almost impossible to believe, but I too possessed her cute looks when I was young. If anyone dared harm this sweet child, no matter the reason, I would kill them without hesitation.

'I'm a little confused about something,' I say, placing my middle finger on the depression in my forehead. 'Am I understanding this correctly? There are so many terrible things happening right now, so many people suffering. This is no time to escape into novels or fiction. We should turn on the TV, watch the news, and confront reality. Right? But no matter what kind of news it is, even a documentary or something like that, it's just one small version of the truth, right? So not all that much different to a novel, don't you think?'

'One small version of the truth?'

'Call it one bigger version of the truth, if you want. I suppose the news has a larger following than most novels. It certainly does have more influence on the world, so maybe the news really is a bigger version of the truth.'

'What are you talking about? You're not telling me you've become one of those lame conspiracy theorists?'

'I don't think I'm a supporter of any particular theory or doctrine.'

'Then what *are* you, Mum?' my daughter demands in annoyance, sweeping her long, dark hair behind her back.

Asked to define myself, I rack my brain to find the most accurate words.

'I'm someone who wants to talk about novels with her daughter. I know there's a twenty-something-year age gap between us, but I want to make an effort to communicate, to find a topic we're both interested in.'

'First of all, news and fiction are two completely different things,' my daughter insists. 'News reflects reality as it is – it's *true*. Novels are nothing but lies. They're not objective, they're not real – they're just written by authors picking out their favourite words and sentences and writing about their own personal fantasies. They're completely disconnected from reality.'

'Do you think so?'

'You're crazy, Mum.'

'I wonder… Are they so different?'

'Any normal adult would see how insane this is.'

'I think the reason we're not seeing eye to eye is because we don't have the same shared assumptions. For you, lies are the opposite of truth, and dreams are the opposite of reality. Fiction is the opposite of nonfiction, and bad is the opposite of good. Right? I'm sorry you have to speak Japanese with me, which I know you're not very strong in, but in my brain's language area, those words aren't so neatly divided. So when you say things like "absolutely" or "obviously", I just don't follow. I suppose that's what you consider "strange", but I just can't help it. Because I'm an "airhead", and I didn't get the special education you did… Yes, like bacon and eggs.'

Suddenly remembering the breakfast my daughter had left untouched this morning, I rise to my feet, pull the plastic container from the fridge, adjust the plastic wrap a little, and put it in the microwave, returning to my seat with a slightly overheated plate of bacon and eggs. All throughout this, my daughter remains unmoving, sitting at the table hands clasped in front of her as she follows me with an unreadable look.

'Um, we got a little sidetracked, didn't we? I was trying to answer your question. What was it again?

Something about a war tomorrow…?'

'I said you'd still be talking about novels even if a huge war broke out tomorrow.'

'Yes, that was it. Can I ask you the opposite question? If people kept on saying there was some benefit to having a war, would you take them seriously? I'm sure your generation wouldn't fall for such a ridiculous argument, right? But it wasn't like that in the past. People were serious enough to risk their lives, and they believed if they fought, if they killed each other enough, if they won, something good would come out of it. It's hard to imagine now, but back then, war was a huge, huge story. But there isn't a story on this earth everyone likes. Even the biggest masterpieces get negative reviews every now and then. Take Dazai Osamu, for instance. You know Dazai Osamu, right? I don't think he really bought into those big stories everyone else believed in. Maybe his head was filled with better stories. When was it written? 1938? 1939? If it was 1939, Japan was already at war with China, and an even bigger one was just about to start. People were dying in huge numbers. It was no time to be talking about novels. But that's the terrible world *Schoolgirl* was written in, you know? He went out of his way to write a novel based on a young girl's diary. And now, almost a century later, it feels like it's overlooking the biggest story of them all, right? But at least you and I have read it, haven't we? So I don't think it's completely meaningless to talk about novels, even on a day when a war is about to begin… Does that answer your question?'

I watch my daughter sitting there in open-mouthed silence, as if having come to a realisation. Just as I reach out to grab a moist sushi roll between my thumb and forefinger, she jumps to her feet and storms out the room without making a sound. I would have preferred not to eat alone, of course, but my daughter isn't my own personal property, so I do nothing to stop her. My lips curl into a smile as I stare at her empty chair. Then, a second later, an overpoweringly hollow feeling falls over me, like I've merely been talking to myself this whole time.

By the way, what do you think the most common word in this book is? I haven't counted them properly or anything, but read it and you'll know – it's 'Mum'.

The protagonist's diary is filled with parts talking about her mother. I feel like if I were to turn it upside down and shake it, her mum might actually fall right out. If I were its editor, I would have changed the title from *Schoolgirl* to *Mother*, because it's always 'Mum this', 'Mum that'. Basically, when you read it, you'll see the word 'mum' again and again and again. The word keeps piling down like snowflakes that refuse to melt, and by the time you reach the last page, you'll feel like you've got it all over your body, and you'll think: 'Right, I've got to take care of my mum.' I felt like I *was* the schoolgirl. And for some reason, that made me, like, super sad. Or maybe not *sad*, exactly – *empty*, more like. I felt like crying, to put it simply. Why do girls, why do daughters, always think about their mums like this? I couldn't get that question out of my head. Technology changes, people's values change, but girls keep on loving their mums in exactly the same way. What I'm feeling now isn't much different to what people thought a hundred years ago. It'd make you feel empty, too, realising how little progress there's been after all this time, and that it'll probably still be like this a hundred years from now.

If I had to honestly put all these thoughts bouncing around my head into words, I think the word 'mum' would come up more times than I could count. Lately, I can't even sleep at night out of worry, imagining what my life would be like without her. I'd be in trouble without my dad, as well, but he's strong, so I don't worry about him so much. My mum, though – it's like she could just disappear without the slightest warning. I'm scared of losing her. I know I go on and on about utilitarianism and altruism, but deep down, maybe I don't really care about anyone except my mum. The world's full of all these problems someone needs to step in and solve, and there are millions and millions of people waiting to be pulled from poverty, and famine, and forced labour, and all that. But in the end, it's my one and only mum I worry about the most. You know the trolley problem, right? If that was real, if for some reason, I had to pick between sacrificing five strangers or losing my mum, I would probably go the selfish route and save my mum first. It's really embarrassing to admit. I know in my mind all lives are equal, and there's no logical reason why my mum's life ought to be more special than those of five other people. But all the same, I just want my mum to be safe. I hate myself for feeling this way. I'd rather just forget the word 'mum' even exists. If I stopped saying it, if my mum stopped being my mum, if I stopped being her daughter, what would she be? What would *I* be?

With my daughter gone, not a single word remains in my body. Feeling like a wisp of smoke on the cusp of disappearing, I shove the leftover bacon and eggs into my mouth in an attempt to overcome the hollow emptiness that has settled over me. Maybe because I haven't had a proper meal since morning, my appetite resurfaces, and I devour the sushi meant for my daughter like a ravenous dog. Nourishment from living creatures slowly seeps into my famished body.

I press the hot water button to prepare the bath, and twenty minutes later, I'm dozing off naked in the thirty-eight-degree water. I love nothing better than floating in the bathtub after eating, dizzy, drowsy, sluggishly heavy, all my blood concentrated in my stomach. The satiety centre in my brain starts sending out signals, flooding me with a burst of serotonin. Filled with this limitless feeling of happiness, my thoughts turn to those unfortunate souls the world over. When I can afford to, I allow myself to feel sorry for others, and at such times, I'm enraptured, considering myself virtuous, kind. There are so many unhappy individuals in the world. Till the day I die, there will never be a shortage of suffering. No matter how many donations charitable organisations might collect, so long as humanity continues to procreate, new misfortunes will keep on entering the world. It could be anyone – but today, for some reason, I want to sympathise with people stricken by severe taste disorders. Of course, there are countless disorders out there more severe in terms of physical pain, but right now, the thought of being unable to taste anything at all seems truly horrifying. Meals consumed merely to survive, so that one's vital functions don't cease to operate – it's incredibly unsettling. There are a great many people, I suspect, who continue to thrive because of the sheer variety of food they eat. I'm one of them. Yesterday, I had noodles, so today, maybe I'll cook rice. If it gets cold tomorrow, we can have hot pot. By deceiving myself over and over making the subtlest of changes to my meals, I can prolong my life and tell myself I'm happy.

That alone is more than enough, but it doesn't have to be all. After leaving the bathroom, I take a tub of Godiva ice cream, a punnet of strawberries, and a bottle of champagne from the refrigerator, savouring the flavours one at a time. The aroma of the cocoa blends perfectly with the sweet and sour tang of the fruit, directly sparking my brain's reward system. I'm happy. I've become the very concept of happiness. At that moment, my phone lights up on the kitchen table. I don't have to look at the screen to know it's my daily ten-o'clock reminder – 'Did you raise a hand against her today?' I tap the *No* button.

Leaning back into the sofa, I call out to AI. 'I don't want to hear any news until after I wake up tomorrow. No alarm, either.'

'News notifications have been disabled. Message notifications have been disabled. The alarm tomorrow morning has been disabled… Are you tired, by any chance? Would you like to listen to some music?'

'No… No, actually, I will. Play some music.'

Music begins playing from the smart speaker, but the slow songs no doubt chosen to soothe a tired mind at the end of the day aren't at all to my liking. I end up asking for 60s jazz music instead, but even after skipping a dozen or so songs, I still can't find one that matches my mood, and so I specify an 80s dream pop album by a British rock band. I focus my attention on the lyrics and melody, neither of which ever fail to move me, on the sweet scent of sandalwood incense, on the complex flavours filling my mouth, and on the beautiful reverberations of Robin Guthrie's guitar, all of it blending together as one. Ah, it's nice. This will be the last of these happy days – because tomorrow, without a doubt, I will hear one way or another the latest tragic news. Perhaps I should try dozing off in the living room to the sound of music? If I sleep somewhere else, I reason, I might be able to ward off the nightmares. And so I place two thin cushions together and slide them under my head.

Just as I'm about to slip into unconsciousness, I hear my daughter's footsteps. She stands there, looking down at me, wondering if I'm awake – and feeling her presence on my skin, her body seems larger than usual, while my own has become that much smaller.

'Who is *you*?' she asks. She speaks hesitantly, just in case I'm already asleep.

I could have chosen not to respond, but in the end – '*You*?' I ask back with my eyes still closed.

'It says "you", at the end of *Schoolgirl*. Just once. "You're the one who is to blame."'

I try to remember what expression my long-lost friend had on her face all those years ago. Come to think of it, I remember trying to figure out who 'you' was supposed to be as well. Right. Once upon a time, she said 'you' all of a sudden, leaving me startled and confused. But right now, I'm too tired to think about the scene or context in which that line occurs. I wish my daughter could have included the sentences before and after.

'And when that happened, everyone would say – ' my daughter reads, the faint sound of paper scraping against paper tickling my ears.

'And when that happened, everyone would say, "Oh, if only she had lived a little longer, she would have figured it out." How saddened they would all be. But if those people were to think about it from our perspective, and see how we had tried to endure despite how terribly painful it was, and how we had even tried to listen carefully, as hard as we could, to what the world might have to say, they would see that, in the end, the same bland lessons were always being repeated over and over, you know, well, merely to appease us. And they would see how we always experienced the same embarrassment of being ignored…'

Her voice, coming out in short fragments, strikes my head like the rhythmic fall of rain. I wish my daughter would read to me like this every night before I go to sleep. Feeling myself drifting away, I gather my last ounces of strength to ask: 'Who do you think *you* is?'

'I don't know. What about you, Mum?'

'Let's talk about it again tomorrow. In the morning.'

'Yeah.'

I think I've rambled a bit too long today. I guess it's going to take me a bit of time to get used to doing these in Japanese. I want to end with at least one useful piece of information, though. Like I mentioned earlier, I get these anxiety attacks when I go to bed, and I don't sleep all that well. Recently, though, I've started making some small changes to get some rest more easily, so I'll share this method I've learned.

Before going to bed, I usually spend some time in my room thinking about ideas for new videos and editing the one I'm working on. When I'm done shooting, all I want to do is turn the camera off and crawl into bed. But before that, I've got to set my alarm for seven o'clock...and then I remember I've got to get up early to upload the video, so I decide to set it to six-thirty even if I end up hitting the snooze button in the morning. I'll put my phone screen down near my pillow so notifications don't keep me awake, close the curtains to block out the light, and try to plunge the room into pitch darkness. Then, when I get into bed and close my eyes, first my mind is strangely clear, but then these random thoughts start flooding it, keeping me up. You know, like what would I do if my mum weren't around anymore? What was I born for? Why *me* and not someone else? Will I stop having these thoughts when I grow up? If everyone eventually disappears anyway, what's the point of the present moment? All sorts of questions, all sorts of thoughts, the same things everyone else has been wondering for a hundred years – they all rise to the surface, and it's suffocating. I tell myself this isn't good, that it's disrupting my sleep – and all that does is make me feel even more anxious. So recently, I've been trying to remove myself from my thoughts as much as possible. To completely forget I'm me.

You're thinking it sounds difficult, right? But there's a trick to it. First, you've got to imagine you're someone else, and really concentrate on that person. The important thing is they've got to be someone who knows how to write. It can be any kind of writing – a diary, stories, even a novel, anything will do so long as they're writing something. You imagine them writing at a desk in a room on a cold rainy day, or sitting down in a crowded café, or surrounded by strangers on a train swaying side to side. You picture them holding a pen, tapping on a keyboard, or gripping their phone in their left hand – you picture it so strongly it's like a dull, numb sensation at the back of your eyes. Then, this is what you tell yourself: 'I'm a character in whatever this person is writing. My body, my mind, my thoughts – this writer is in control of everything I am.'

'Good night.' As soon as you think that, as soon as your writer puts those words to the page, adding commas and full stops and whatever, you cease to be you, becoming just a new paragraph on a blank piece of paper. At that point, you're as good as asleep, waiting for your next awakening…

All right guys, that's all for today's video. Thanks for watching. I hope you all enjoyed it. I'll see you all again in the next one. Good night, sweet dreams. Bye-bye.

BAD MUSIC

I was meditating in the prep room when my ears registered a sound I simply couldn't ignore, prompting my eyes to snap wide open.

I had been able to make out voices through my headphones for the past few minutes, so I knew people were outside. It wasn't unusual for students who didn't know I was just next door to sneak into the music room without permission. Every now and then, some sleep-deprived kid would come here hoping to get some shut-eye, while on other days, bored troublemakers might think to play around on the piano. Students with all sorts of problems liked to frequent the music room. Every time I heard the door slide open unexpectedly, I considered rewriting the 'Access Prohibited Except for Classes' sign in larger letters. Then again, a few years ago, I tried changing the font face to make it easier to read, but that did nothing to improve the situation. The issue probably wasn't that students couldn't read the sign – more that they weren't *inclined* to read it.

There was only the one sound, and it wasn't particularly loud – certainly not enough to distract from my meditative focus. It was just the bang of two objects colliding, that was all. Yet ordinary though it was, I couldn't let it go unnoticed. Given the weight of the collision, it sounded like something might have been damaged – and part of me suspected it was the result of deliberate force. After all, I would be neglecting my responsibilities if I turned a blind eye when a student took to damaging school property. Of course, I wasn't psychic, and this was all just a hunch on my part – but my intuition hadn't failed me yet so far as sound was concerned.

As such, I removed my headphones, put on my glasses, and rose to my feet, bumping my little toe on the taiko drum stand as I opened the door to the music room. My guess, it turned out, had mostly been on the mark – only it wasn't damaged school equipment this time around. Rather, there were two boys in the room, one of them lying injured on the floor, blood running down his face.

'Ah,' I sighed in tired recognition.

Yes, that was the first word to slip out of my mouth.

I distinctly remember that first 'Ah'. When I told the story later, however, I found myself making various small adjustments.

'I was organising some documents in the prep room when I heard this loud noise over in the music room. Worried, I went to take a look, when I found Omi bleeding. I was caught off guard, and I rushed over. "Are you okay?" I asked. I was so flustered I forgot to ask Fujiwara what happened, but my first priority was attending to Omi's injury, so I helped him to the infirmary.'

I was in charge of music classes for all grade levels at this middle school, so I recognised the students' faces. To tell the truth, however, their names didn't immediately jump to mind. The one still standing wore a surprised look, while the other was flat on his back on the ground, scrunching his face up in pain while clutching at the base of his neck. It was clear from one glance that violence had taken place here, and I had no difficulty visualising the one punching the other in the face, sending him falling backward to hit his head on a desk. Yes, that was a safe assumption given that one desk was out of alignment with the others. Both students had that still-underdeveloped physique typical of middle school boys, but the one on his feet looked to be the stronger of the pair.

I knelt on the floor next to the fallen student, peering into his pain-racked face. 'Ow…' he muttered weakly, a thin trickle of blood leaking down his lips.

'Can you stand?' I called out. 'Can you walk to the infirmary?'

Far from responding, however, the boy continued to weep, his tears mingling with his blood.

I glanced up at the other student. 'Hey. What's going on here…?'

He didn't seem interested in talking to me. In fact, he seemed taken aback by this unexpected turn of events, his voice stuck in his throat. No doubt he hadn't expected a teacher to walk in on them like this.

Sandwiched between these two mute students, I turned my attention to the silence hovering over the music room in the late afternoon light – and as I listened, I found myself wondering if I had remembered to pause the music on my headphones. Deflated by that thought, I grabbed the fallen student by the arm and somewhat heavy-handedly pulled him to his feet.

'Come on, stand up. It's not like your leg's broken.'

I held the boy with my fingertips so as not to get any blood on my own clothes and led him to the infirmary.

At first, he maintained his wordless crying, but by the time we carefully navigated the staircase to the ground floor, he was muttering under his breath in an angry, guttural voice: 'Fuck Fujiwara.' 'I'll kill him.' 'He's dead.'

Once we reached the infirmary, we walked in on the school nurse, eating lunch in her white coat. The moment she laid eyes on us, she let out a loud wail, spat the food from her mouth, and dashed over with a terrified look.

'Hey, what happened?!' she demanded. 'Blood! You're bleeding! You – you've got to put some pressure on it! Sit down there! You didn't hit your head, did you?!'

The nurse was visibly distressed by all the blood, but that didn't stop her from setting about her duties quickly and efficiently. With seamless movements, she took a towel from the shelf, moistened a piece of gauze with an antiseptic solution, retrieved an icepack from a small refrigerator and filled it with ice, then wiped the student's mouth with the towel.

'That must have hurt,' she said comfortingly. 'Don't worry, you'll be fine. You're bleeding a little, but the cut isn't too deep. Cuts like that tend to bleed a lot. It must have come as a bit of a shock, I'm sure. It'll stop soon, so there's no need to stress.'

There was something reassuring about the nurse's figure, as plump and round as a loaf of bread, and her faintly defined facial contours. Even the injured student, looking genuinely surprised to have met an adult bothered by the sight of so much blood, seemed to breathe a sigh of relief. With his wounds disinfected, his eyes, until just a brief moment ago burning with hatred and a thirst for revenge, suddenly cooled.

Later that day, Omi underwent a more thorough examination at a local clinic. His injury wasn't overly serious, but I knew what to expect – and sure enough, I was soon assigned additional work outside of my regular duties.

To begin with, I was called to a meeting with both the 'victim', Omi, and the 'perpetrator', Fujiwara, their parents, and their homeroom teachers (they were both in their second year, albeit different classes), as well as the head of the faculty, to give my 'testimony' as the 'primary eyewitness' and the first adult to arrive at the 'scene'. It was the head of the faculty, a man I secretly cursed with the moniker 'old bastard', who came up with all these absurd terms. Whenever I used a more down-to-earth description like 'the music room' or called the student simply by his name, he wouldn't hesitate to jump in and stop me: 'You mean the *scene*, yes?' 'That would be the *victim*, Omi, no?'

Not only did he force us all to take part in this nauseating mock detective drama of his, the old bastard even made me attend a hastily arranged 'discussion' with the students. 'A discussion', he stubbornly insisted, 'is first and foremost between the students' homeroom teachers and their parents. But without the primary eyewitness, there can be no discussion.' His argument, though, didn't have a shred of sense to it. I didn't need to be there for him to simply convey my so-called testimony to the kids' parents. No big deal, you might think. It should only take me a minute or so to get my account of the event off my chest. But constantly working with all these kids aged twelve to fifteen year in, year out – well, it messes with your head, blinding you to reason and logic. Since the first day I started teaching at this school, I hadn't failed to notice my coworkers all had a screw or two loose. To be honest, I no longer found the pantomime all that shocking.

The 'discussion' was held in the audio-visual room, which was the only air-conditioned room in the whole school outside the staffroom and the infirmary. Even though it was already mid-September, the other classrooms were simply too hot to invite parents into. In the end, the 'discussion' was made up of Omi and Fujiwara, their mothers, their homeroom teachers, the head of the faculty, the vice principal, and me. While we teachers and the students waited inside the audio-visual room, the first mother strolled in, her shoes clacking against the floor. Outside of a student play, never before had I heard someone express such pent-up anger through the sound of high heels. Given that she was making no effort to hide her indignation, this was no doubt Omi's mother, not Fujiwara's. And indeed, it was – her face was strikingly similar to her fourteen-year-old son's. They could have been mistaken for twins, and with their expressions, they were both playing the role of the victim to a T.

'We would like to express our sincerest apologies,' we teachers said as a chorus.

Without betraying any reaction, the woman sat down in the chair offered by the vice principal and pulled the lever to set it at an appropriate height. Once she found a comfortable position, she covered her face below the eyes with both hands and remained as still as a silkworm cocoon. You could have been forgiven for thinking she was trying to take in the scent of her palms. No one dared ask what she was doing, so I couldn't say for sure, but I suspected she couldn't bear the stench wafting across from the old bastard seated next to her. Even with the air-conditioning turned on high, his body odour must have come as a kick in the gut to anyone not used to choking on it in the staffroom on a daily basis.

Only when the other mother arrived a full five minutes after the scheduled time did the woman remove her hands and speak up. 'Who do you think you are, making us wait?' she demanded.

I was impressed by the unexpected vocal quality. Her voice resonated clearly, like that of someone who had mastered diaphragmatic breathing, and there was a pleasant intonation to her assertive way of speaking. It seemed that I, however, was the only one who saw her voice in a favourable light.

'I'm so sorry,' Fujiwara's mum whispered timidly – but only after letting out a terrified hiccup. This went beyond merely being weak-minded – she was so pathetic, all but falling apart at the seams, that I literally felt sorry for her. But even with his mother taking the blame for his own outburst, slumping in her chair, Fujiwara himself seemed unfazed, calmly folding his arms on the desk in front of him.

From that point on, Omi's mother took centre stage. I suspected she was well-accustomed to issuing instructions, and she naturally assumed control of the situation. Indeed, while the head of the faculty had prepared a written summary of the incident in advance of the 'discussion', it ultimately lay untouched on the table.

I kept to myself throughout, until –

‘Your turn,’ our de facto boss said, pointing to me – and so I launched into the script I had committed to memory ahead of time.

‘I was organising some documents in the prep room,’ I began, ‘when I heard this loud noise over in the music room…’

Once I was finished, I sat back and observed, no more involved in the ‘discussion’ than a piece of wallpaper. All that was left for me to do was to *listen* – listen to the sterile pursuit of ‘responsibility’, listen to everyone root around for the ostensible ‘cause’, listen to the ‘shocking truth’ that underlay the dispute between the two boys. In short, Fujiwara hit Omi because a certain female student he was dating was two-timing him. With this new revelation thrown into the mix, the ‘discussion’ was prolonged considerably. The adults all tried to coax out the name of the mysterious femme fatale, but both boys, perhaps hoping to protect the identity of their crush, refused to divulge her name.

I had to stop myself from remarking out loud that my fellow teachers were acting as if this were some stupid detective game, while the students themselves seemed to be playing the main characters in a soppy melodrama. When did this place turn into a drama school again? It was around that time I started rhyming behind closed lips, finding pairs with the word most often repeated within the walls of this unending 'discussion'. 'Responsibility / impossibility / credibility / comprehensivity / accountability / volatility / vulnerability / plausibility.'

Who's responsible? Who's going to take responsibility? *Someone* has to be responsible. Who is it?

'Who's gonna take responsibility? / In the discussion room, check the possibility. / Nine deep in the crowd, a tight density, / Full crew, but this scene's just nonsense, see? / Guys loving two-timing gals with ease / No defence when fists fly, it's a tease. / Pretentious parents with their dumb decrees.

'Unrestrained, emotions untamed, / Hushing the Sick Kids, lust inflamed. / Banned from the music room, they roam, / No mercy for monkeys, not a bone. / Funky monkeys locked away, no bail, / Jocks suited for sports clubs, that's their tale.

'Who's gonna bear the load, who'll take the blame? / Patch up the wounds, try to stop the pain. / On the Keihin-Tōhoku line, what about my train? / Public servants, PTA members – '

At that moment, the boss interrupted my rhyming. 'Hey, you. What do you think you're doing? You're the music teacher, right? What exactly do you think is so funny?'

Having fully tuned into the rhyming, I snapped back to reality and glanced around the room. The others had worked themselves up into such a frenzy without me, and now they were all staring my way. What the hell was going on? I hurried to reorient myself in the conversation. Once the confusion about the two-timing girl was out of the way, Omi's mother had taken out a handful of medical receipts and started going on about compensation. I hadn't caught the exact amounts, but it wasn't like I had covered my ears, so I still got the basic flow of the exchange. I just couldn't understand why I, a complete outsider in this situation, was suddenly the centre of attention.

The boss wasn't just staring at me – she had turned her whole body in my direction.

'You,' she bellowed. 'You… You think this is funny?'

'Not at all,' I murmured, wringing my voice out of my neck. To my own astonishment, that was the best I could muster.

'What are you smirking about, then?'

'I'm not smirking.'

'You were smiling. You think this is a joke?'

'No. Um. No I wasn't.'

'Don't take me for an idiot. I saw you.'

'I wasn't. Really,' I insisted, shifting my gaze to Fujiwara, seated directly in front of me.

The boss's seat was some distance from mine, so the angle or a trick of the lighting must have made it look like I was laughing. Fujiwara, I thought, would know the truth, so I appealed to him with my eyes. 'I wasn't smiling, was I?' But he just stared back dispassionately, with a swagger like some rich family's pampered puppy. For some reason, staring into those cold eyes, I thought to myself: 'This kid has a cute face.'

The boss glared at me for a further ten seconds, but pursued the matter no further, clicking her tongue in frustration as she turned back to the topic of her son's medical expenses.

After putting in several hours of overtime and even more in emotional labour, the incident in the music room was brought to a close, and I was left having to deal with the blood stains in the music room. I hesitated over asking to see if the school janitor could clean them up, but in the end, I decided to bring my own stain remover from home and do it myself.

Unlike the regular classrooms, the music room was fitted with soundproof carpeting. It was probably a little unreasonable to ask a fourteen-year-old kid to keep that in mind when picking a fight with a fellow student, but I wished the two had given at least a passing thought to how difficult blood would be to remove from the floor. Or at the very least, the person who had ended up causing the stain in the first place should be the one to remove it. But Fujiwara refused to respond in any way. Even in class, not only did he avoid making eye contact with me, he had stopped doing his alto recorder practice. I couldn't fathom what he and Omi had been thinking. If they wanted to fight, they ought to have at least waited until after school hours. If they had roughed each other up outside of the school grounds, the incident could have been resolved so much more easily.

In the end, I had to cut my precious meditation time short to scribble out a list of several 'should-do' tasks and crawl along the floor of the music room, spraying stain remover on fibres soaked with brown blood and scrubbing them down with a soaking towel. Each time the cloth hit the floor, it sounded like I was stomping on a bass drum at a speed of 246 BPM. The stain had been left untouched for two whole days, but with each slap of the towel, the colour slowly ebbed away, the grey carpet fading to white. Yet even after the blood was all but unnoticeable, I didn't slow my beat. Focusing to keep the time, I let Queen's *Stone Cold Crazy* play in my head. I only realised how angry I was when the pain in my hands started approaching unbearable levels. Forcing them to stop, I tossed the towel aside, moved from a crawling position to a Zen posture, and took a slow, deep breath.

If I was bristling, there were countless reasons for it. In which case, I ought to try to change my thinking. The entire universe was interconnected, and no single event was solely responsible for any given outcome. As such, the root cause of my resentment could perhaps be traced back to my high school days, or else to when I first decided to make my way as a middle school teacher, or even to the electrical stimulation of the hypothalamus that drove Fujiwara to commit his act of violence, which itself went back to the structure of the human body more generally. The universe was one. We were one with the universe. The universe and my anger were one. Everything was one, and one was everything. Focus on your breath, feel the energy of the universe, take in the energy of the earth, and turbocharge the energy of life.

But no matter how much I tried, I lacked the patience to bring my mind around to such a spiritual mental state. I just didn't care about life energy or anything of the sort – all I wanted was to rent a studio and hammer away mindlessly on a real drum set. Eventually, my vague mental image of the universe gave way to a more concrete one – Omi's mother.

'Maybe I'll punch you in the face, too,' I said out loud as the words came to me, but even hearing them resound in my own ears, I still wasn't sure if this was genuine anger.

Sae was already there when I got back to my apartment after my relentless beating of the music room floor. She had already cooked a meal for the two of us, and was waiting for me to get home before digging in. It had been almost two weeks since I had last seen her.

Sae was an artist two years my senior, and we had been housemates ever since I joined the workforce. She wasn't a 'self-proclaimed' artist or an illustrator or anything like that. No, she made her living creating real, genuine artworks – abstract paintings in the style of Mark Rothko, to be precise. Whenever she had a solo exhibition somewhere in Tōkyō, I would be sure to attend. As her friend, I hoped to someday be able to understand her works, but to be perfectly honest, I had no idea when they might finally dawn on me. I could tell she must possess exceptional talent to be able to make a living from abstract paintings, but that was the best I could say without stretching credibility. Living with an artist hadn't really sharpened my sensibilities in any noticeable way.

We sat in different parts of the living room eating the salad she had thrown together, updating each other on recent events. She originally had the apartment to herself, so there was only one chair at the small dining table, which meant that if we were going to eat at the same time, one of us would have to sit on the couch. There was plenty of space, but so far, we hadn't discussed whether or not to buy another chair. Sae also rented a studio complete with its own bathroom, so she spent half the month away from home. Neither of us felt the need to actually face the other while eating, which was one of very few traits we shared.

When I told her about the incident at work, Sae doubled over on the couch in laughter. '*Did* you smile?' she asked.

'I told you, no,' I insisted, pouring a miniature bottle of cheap sparkling wine into a souvenir mug Sae had picked up at one place or another. 'No way I'd do that. I'm not *completely* devoid of common sense, you know?'

'Then why did she get so pissed off at you?'

'Ms Clacking High Heels thought she saw something she didn't. Probably just a shadow falling over my face or something. That's all.'

Sae had laughed so hard that her wine was dribbling down her chin, forcing her to grab a tissue to dab it away. She tended to go all out when she cracked up, looking like her head and chin were being crushed together, as if she could literally die of laughter. Her facial expressions were rich and varied – a sharp contrast from what you would naturally expect based on the quiet style of her artworks. Seriously, I had never seen her with a blank look on her face. Even her driver's licence photo showed her with a barely concealed half-smile.

'But you know, sometimes people's emotions come out naturally, even if you don't mean to smile,' she pointed out.

'I mean, it *was* funny. Just think about it – seven adults being run ragged by a pair of bratty hormone-crazed middle school kids.'

'It's so *emo*,' Sae muttered, her skinny frame squirming about as she held a cushion to her stomach.

To her, most everything seemed too emotional, filled with excitement and passion. Perhaps that was a necessary quality for an artist, but sometimes, I found myself tiring of her hypersensitivity. No, it wasn't just tiredness that came over me – rather, more a complex mix of exhaustion and sympathy.

'Hormone-crazed middle school kids, huh? Maybe I'll use that idea as the basis for my next picture?' she wondered out loud.

'Why don't you? You could call it *The Awakening*.'

'Huh. That's pretty good. I like it... *The Awakening*...' Sae murmured as if jotting down ideas in her head. Then, she stood up from the couch, pulled a large casserole dish from the oven, and carefully scooped a serving of rice gratin onto my plate. 'I knew I was in good hands getting a music teacher as a housemate. You can stay here forever, you know? It'd do wonders for my artistic career. I don't care how much you trash the place, I won't raise the rent on you.'

'Suppose I *had* smiled,' I said, redirecting the conversation away from my turning the apartment upside down. 'What would be so bad about that? It's not like I said anything to disrupt the conversation. And even if I *did* smile, it would be so faint, like on the *Mona Lisa*.'

'That much? I can see why that would be inappropriate. Someone might think you're mocking them. I've seen the *Mona Lisa* at the Louvre, and let me tell you, she looks so much sassier in person. I'll bet she was pretty nasty in real life. Really, I wonder why she's smiling like that?'

Sae reached for her iPad propped up on the TV stand. Quickly rubbing her fingers across the screen, she brought up an image of the *Mona Lisa*, fixing her disagreeable visage with a stern, professional stare. I peered across at the screen while letting a spoonful of gratin cool in my mouth. The high-resolution image faithfully reproduced even the cracks in the canvas and the work's age-related deterioration. There she was, the *Mona Lisa*, covered in cracks and looking like an old lady strolling the streets of Shinjuku, trying to hide her wrinkly face with a smattering of foundation smeared across her skin.

'Maybe the mum of that hormone-crazed kid has a good eye for this sort of thing? Da Vinci-level powers of observation, the ability to read subtle nuances that fly over most ordinary people's heads. I mean, take a look at this,' Sae teased as she handed me her iPad.

I pulled a second small bottle of sparkling wine from the fridge, poured it into my mug, and at Sae's urging, glanced at the unceasing stream of *Mona Lisa* images that she pulled down from the internet.

The world's most famous portrait had been parodied countless times over by later generations of artists, and the myriad variations made a perfect way to pass the time over a good drink. There were parody works which served as T-shirt designs, even a tattoo inked into a rapper's neck. Perusing the many faces of these Mona Lisas, the works reflecting equal parts respect and sacrilege, I came across an interesting description: 'The enigmatic smile of the woman in the *Mona Lisa* has been the subject of much debate. Though today, her smile is often described as innocent or charming, in medieval Europe, where power was concentrated in the hands of the Christian faith, smiles were considered indecent or else characteristic of mental disturbance, and people went about their lives keeping their emotions carefully under wraps.'

I tried to imagine the medieval European landscape in which Leonardo Da Vinci must have lived. Whether you stop in a town square or a meeting hall, there isn't a single person smiling. Everyone just walks down the street with these tense looks on their faces. It reminded me of the morning subway rush here in modern Japan. What would happen if, in this era, smiles were once again prohibited, and people started going about their whole lives acting like subway passengers? To begin with, the value of smiles had undergone a complete one-eighty at some point between medieval Europe and the present day. These days, no one would think you're mentally disturbed just for smiling. On the contrary, it was part of basic social etiquette to wear a smile-like expression when meeting and greeting people, and failing to do so carried a huge risk of leaving a negative impression or damaging the trust you were hoping to establish.

Right, it undermined trust. Poor facial expressions and a lack of emotion were what gave people the impression there was something defective in you. That was why people went so far as to put wires in their mouths for twenty months on end to forge a well-defined smile. Yet the concept of a smile in modern society was more complex – it wasn't just a matter of pulling up the edges of your mouth to show your teeth. People were capable of instantly analysing the overall balance of your face to determine if it was a genuine smile, a forced one, a smirk, a sneer, or something else entirely. It was as if your facial expressions could reveal everything about you – right down to your inner self and personality. But why had humans developed such a depth of emotion? If all we needed was to survive and reproduce, there would be no need for so many different kinds of smiles.

I stared up at the ceiling, rotating the mug held up to my mouth to lap up any wine left stuck at the bottom. As the sweet aroma dissolved into my saliva and washed over my tongue, I arrived at a hypothesis.

Theory: The source of this expansion of human emotions lay in artists, such as musicians and painters. I could probably also include poets and novelists in that category. These sensitive individuals, the so-called 'creative types', were the first to discover human emotion was something that could be commodified. In the pursuit of creating more emotionally-charged works that resonated with people's hearts, they set out to delve into new, uncharted territories of feeling. Music and fine art were capable of expressing emotions to some extent, while novelists could give names to previously unknown ones. And once these unknown emotions were conceptualised and popularised, later generations of creatives expanded on them in their own works, further developing and reinforcing them. Without literature and art, perhaps the human psyche would have developed along very different lines?

If this hypothesis was correct, then what we regarded as human emotion was ultimately no more than a pattern of behaviour, a mental construct that we all acquired from existing media and cherry-picked from for our own use. The way Omi's mother had clicked her high heels was a perfect example. In her mind, she wasn't actually experiencing a process called 'anger', nor was her body reacting to it to create that sound. Rather, she was simply embodying a heel clack that she had received from some external stimulus in order to match the performative emotions and attitude of 'a mother whose son has been injured'. Fujiwara's tragic punch was also the result of mistaking his own emotions for the pre-learned behaviour of 'a man gone mad with rage after losing his girlfriend'. In the modern age, the diversity and multiplicity of these constructed minds was seen in a positive light, as proof of someone's 'breadth of character' or 'richness of personality'. And conversely, someone who lacked emotion was seen as boring, flawed, unworthy of trust.

But once you took emotion out of the equation, weren't all expressions just particular movements of the muscles that comprised the human face? How could simple muscle movements have any real relation to people's personalities?

The last thing I looked up on the iPad that night was a workshop on facial expression training. Lost in my reflection of facial expressions, I found myself filling out the registration form without even meaning to. Just as I hit the submit button, the iPad's battery ran out.

'Where's the charger?' I asked, looking up – realising only then that Sae had already left the room. Without my noticing, she had tidied up the dishes that I had left scattered about, taken a bath, and was now sound asleep in bed with a grim look on her face.

The workshop was held in a shopping centre event room. It was a simple space, much like a typical conference room, equipped with plain office tables and chairs and a whiteboard. A scent diffuser, probably belonging to the workshop instructor, was emitting a cloud of steam while occasionally making low popping sounds.

The thirty or so participants filling the seats all wore what I would describe as *distinct* expressions – so distinct, in fact, that I questioned whether they needed any training at all. Theirs weren't ready-made faces inherited from their parents, but rather 'best-self' expressions constructed over years under clear sets of guidelines. As soon as the women took their seats (the participants were all women), they peered into the mirrors set up on the tables, checking the intensity of their false eyelashes with their fingertips and massaging their necks showing over their low-cut blouses. I hadn't given much thought ahead of time to the kind of people who would be attending the workshop, but I realised now that these women were warriors caught up in a battle against aging. I was the only one with such a low sense of personal beauty as to venture into a shopping centre on a Sunday morning without any makeup on. I could clearly see my face in the mirror, bathed in fluorescent light so bright it made my eyes hurt, looking much older than I remembered. Knowing I wouldn't need to go into work today, I had stayed up late rapping lyrics all night long, and the result was the gaunt countenance staring back at me.

When the instructor entered the room, the gazes of all the women peering into their mirrors turned her way. The participants were impressive enough in their own right, but the instructor's facial expression was unmistakably a world apart. Her well-trained, imposing smile left no room for any hint of personality or inner thought to shine through. Even to the untrained eye, it was clear the way she carried herself had reached a realm far beyond normal facial features or makeup.

The instructor introduced herself, her smile under perfect control. She looked to be in her late thirties and explained that she had retired from a career in the airline industry to become what was called an 'etiquette instructor'. She had been involved in various activities for several years now, from facial muscle training to anti-aging research. Recently, in order to differentiate herself from other facial muscle trainers, she had taken to calling herself a 'happy face creator'. Her PowerPoint presentation projected onto the whiteboard displayed a long list of qualifications and certificates. The workshop proceeded quickly from point to point, with the instructor's presence too overwhelming for me to take everything in as she hurriedly switched slides from 'What is a Good Facial Expression?' to 'How Good Facial Expressions Can Improve Your Life'. Seemingly important catchphrases came and went (platitudes like 'Happiness Can be Learned' and 'No Expression, No Life'), and the participants recited them one after the next. The venue was a stark contrast to the dull classes I held with my shy middle school students – here, everyone was bursting with energy, united as they worked toward a common goal.

Wrapping up her presentation, the instructor went on at length about what horrifying fates awaited us should our facial muscles begin to deteriorate, underscored by a pair of comparative images showing two women on the screen at the front of the room.

'It's obvious when you look at them side by side, see?' the instructor said. The room became slightly less tense as she broke into a smile for the very first time, only for it to quickly melt away, as all of a sudden, she looked to be on the verge of tears.

'Which face looks happier? Needless to say, it's the first one. I don't mean to be rude, but the other doesn't look happy at all. What did you all think when you saw them? Which face would you all like to have? Which one would you rather wear while going about your lives? The answer goes without saying.'

After a short break, we moved on to the actual training. I was left bewildered, however, when the instructor suddenly shouted: 'Let's begin!' Sometime during the ten-minute break, her voice had undergone an abrupt transformation. Perhaps her teaching style involved using different voices for lectures and exercises, as her unremarkable – frankly, quite ordinary – feminine voice had developed deep, resonating bass notes that reverberated through my flesh.

'Empty your mind. Focus on your breathing. Let yourself go. Concentrate on each and every muscle comprising your face.'

The instructor certainly wasn't barefoot, nor was she dressed in a monk's robe – she was wearing ten-centimetre-high heels and a blouse with a ribbon tied to it – yet her tone of voice as she addressed us called to mind that of a meditation instructor. It was made up of monotonous, rhythmic wavelengths, gently lulling me to sleep like Satie's *Trois Gymnopédies*.

For the life of me, I had never been able to properly

understand the music of Satie or Debussy. Whether it was music or paintings, I just couldn't find any hint of meaning in Impressionistic art. Impression? So what? It had never struck me as interesting. Back when I was in primary school, I once spent three days and nights searching for the right set of drums to make the *Trois Gymnopédies* more *listenable*. But now, at long last, I felt like I was beginning to understand Satie. His music wasn't about being interesting or boring, listenable or unlistenable – it was meant to eliminate all other noises occupying your head.

The instructor's voice served as an appropriate trigger, allowing me to fully immerse myself in the training. All other noises faded into the distance, and any sense of unease or shame that might have lingered in my consciousness fell away. I could perceive but three things: the instructor's voice, my expression in the mirror, and my facial muscles.

It never really crossed my mind, but yes, there really were muscles inside my face. As the delicate powers of this face that had long eluded me rose to the surface, one of the participants spoke up with a question: 'Hold on, please. If I pull the corners of my lips up like that, if I stretch my skin and move my muscles like you're saying, won't that actually increase the number of wrinkles? Won't it accelerate the aging process?'

That might be a natural concern for some of the participants, but I wasn't at all interested in the answer, so I turned my attention back to my three points of focus. Calling upon my muscles, lying dormant for longer than I could remember, I pulled the flesh comprising my cheeks to its utmost limits. Inevitably, the face reflected in the mirror was far from beautiful – more like a split-mouthed clown from some horror movie – but I decided to trust in the instructor's wisdom. After all, she had maintained her imposing smile all throughout, the corners of her mouth not drooping by a single millimetre. She had an astonishing command over her own flesh, one that more than made up for the rancid dubiousness of her title as a 'happy face creator'. If I followed her lead, I hoped, I too would be able to take full control over my own flesh.

Once the first series of exercises was over, I was left quietly moved by the pleasant twitching I felt in my cheeks. My mind, clouded by lack of sleep, was suddenly clear, a newfound energy surging through my body. It was a level of enlightenment that went far beyond anything I had been able to attain during my daily lunchtime meditation sessions. Muscles, I realised, were incredibly versatile, with the ability to solve all of life's problems. I had never given much thought to them before. Yes, I had busied myself with thoughts about near enough everything else, but one thing had always been missing: muscles.

The participants filed out of the venue one by one, but my body hadn't yet fully adapted to the new plane of existence I had discovered thanks to these muscles, so I remained glued to my seat. At that moment –

'Um, do forgive me if I'm mistaken,' the instructor said, her hoop earrings swaying side to side as she approached, 'but are you Mitsui Yōji's daughter, by any chance?'

'Hah?' sounded my feeble response.

The instructor's eyes lit up and she gave a squeal like a recently re-stringed violin. 'I knew it! Your name is so impressive, so memorable – I recognised it the minute I saw today's class list. My family and I all *adore* classical music. I've even been to one of your father's concerts...'

She went on and on. She seemed to be very well-informed about my dad's recent activities and was evidently trying to convey with her body and face that she was more than just a superficial fan – that rather, she was a serious aficionado of classical music. If I were my usual self, I might have been able to offer her a proper response, but I had been so busy mentally reviewing the steps of all that face training that her words didn't quite sink in.

'You're not a student right now, are you?' she asked.

'Huh?' I stammered, taken aback by the sudden question and the light touch on my upper arm. 'Um, no. I'm not a student. Huh? You're talking about me, right, not my dad? I graduated from college years ago.'

'You must be performing somewhere, then?' she asked.

'What?'

'I'd love to hear you perform. Do you have any recitals coming up soon?'

'Um. No. I don't really perform in public. Actually, I'm teaching at a middle school.'

'Oh… Why is that?'

The instructor's divine smile never wavered, but she couldn't hide the momentary dark cloud passing over her eyes.

'Why is that? Why did you become a teacher, of all things?'

Whenever someone asked me that question, their voice laced with disappointment, my mind always turned to my four-eyed father.

It was during my senior year of high school. I was at home while my dad was at a hotel somewhere in Europe for work. That day, I was supposed to submit a career outline for homework, so I called him over Skype under the guise of wanting to talk about my future plans. The Wi-Fi at his hotel, however, had been spotty from the very beginning, and while flicking through the brochure outlining various music academies, I struggled to pick up his voice coming through my headphones after a noticeable delay.

'Wow. This one does a music education course,' I said while scanning the pamphlet. It wasn't so much I wanted to share this with my dad – it just slipped out in a moment of surprise. And that exclamation became the very catalyst for my later becoming a teacher in earnest.

Without that pamphlet, I might never have known you could find a job teaching music to middle and high-school students. Music was a mandatory subject, so naturally every school had to offer it, and I vaguely remembered a teacher at my own one waving a conductor's baton about at the front of class. But in my mind, I had never associated that music teacher with an actual profession. Even as a high-school student, I had a tendency to zone out at times – I was completely indifferent to matters of everyday life, and I went about my day thinking about music almost every waking hour. I didn't *hate* schoolwork, but I never took it particularly seriously because I just didn't see how it was relevant. No, the only thing I ever showed an interest in was music. On top of that, I had a strong bias toward the music that interested me. I didn't bother myself worrying about whatever we happened to be covering in music class, or with my dad's work, either.

The figure on the other side of the computer screen failed to respond.

'Dad? Can you hear me?' I called out. 'Dad? Are you listening? Hey, did you know? It says here you can get a teaching licence at a music college. A teaching licence. Do you know anyone who did that? Anyone who decided to become a music teacher at a middle school or a high school? I mean, what do music teachers actually do?'

'Mu…sic…'

My dad's voice grew increasingly choppy, and when finally the image froze altogether, I ended the call and tried redialling. By the time we connected again over a weak signal, he seemed strangely out of sorts.

'Why do you want to be a music teacher of all things?' he asked reproachfully. 'Do you even know what a music teacher does? Since when have you wanted that for yourself? You're still going to play the piano after going to college, I hope?'

'I don't think you heard me properly, Dad,' I corrected him. 'I didn't say I wanted to be a music teacher. I just said they had a music education programme. Did you know you could get a teaching licence at a music college? That's what I was asking.'

'Think very carefully. A teaching licence? What are you going to do with that? What do you think those four years of study at a music college are for? It isn't a game. You can play the piano, compose your own music, do whatever you want. You won't have to worry about finding a job thanks to my connections… But enough of this music teacher nonsense. It's a waste of your potential. A boring job for boring people.'

I felt so refreshed. It wasn't a problem with the internet connection – our voices were simply failing to properly reach each other. Completely by accident, I had brushed up against my dad's real thoughts. It was a shocking experience, but also an uplifting one. I had never known he considered teaching music a boring job for boring people. Never before had I heard him disparage or look down on others like that. And even though it was all because of a simple misunderstanding, this was the first time he had so strongly rejected my own ideas. Ever since I was little, he always let me do whatever I wanted. When I developed a sudden interest in percussion one morning and stopped practicing the piano, he didn't complain. He never intervened when I chose which pieces to play during recitals. My gentle dad, who even laughed out loud and forgave me for playing James Booker's version of Chopin's *Minute Waltz* at an important competition, was only now seriously trying to influence his daughter's decisions.

'But what sort of a bad profession did music teaching have to be, to get my dad all worked up like this?' I was curious, so I said to him: 'You're so mean, Dad. How can you dismiss my dreams like that, without even a second thought? I don't care if you're against it, I'm going to be a music teacher.'

At the time, the role of a 'rebellious teenager refusing to listen to her father' came naturally to me. The only reason I was able to pull it off so easily was because my mum had been watching a soap opera in the living room while we ate dinner not an hour before this scheduled Skype call. In reality, I had never felt particularly dissatisfied in my relationship with my dad. I just hoped that by playing the part of a teenage girl in a soap opera, I could bring out more of his unexpected side.

But the Wi-Fi connection was breaking up again. My dad's voice abruptly cut off, and his low-resolution face on the screen froze, replaced with a blurry mess split into two separate images. In the slightly darker image, he was staring at me with full force, while in the lighter one, his eyes were only half open. I kept up my performance, staring into those four eyes of his and waiting for his voice to come through the headset once again.

I never stopped to ask him if he could actually hear me, but even I found my amateur improvisation simply unbearable to listen to. Yet as I continued to blurt out all the right notes, I found myself slipping into my groove, and I started rambling about 'the anguish of being born the daughter of a world-class musician'. If he had actually been here in the room with me, there would have been no way I could have played out such a cheesy scenario. This was probably some variation of the 'drunken blunders' adults often engaged in, but instead of alcohol, it was the unstable Wi-Fi connection that had loosened my tongue.

In fact, I would go on to make this same mistake several times again later on in life. In my case, it seems that the drunkenness that other people experience after consuming alcohol can be triggered by certain situations involving sound. When I can't make out sounds that ought to be audible or when I can hear things I shouldn't, my ears lose all sense of coordination, and my brain freezes up. My sense of reason goes out of the window as I get caught up in a high, and I can't control my bizarre speech and behaviour. And so, drunk on this addictive rhythm, I found myself criticising the name my dad had given me.

Had he ever paused to consider how much pressure he was putting on me, naming me Sonata? He had basically forced me to learn the piano from the very moment I came into the world. Sure, he wanted me to have a proud career in the music industry – but wasn't it tantamount to child abuse limiting my career choices like that? Would a banker call their kid Account or Deposit? Did Steve Jobs name his daughter Apple or iPhone? That's what you're doing. Don't you think you're glorifying your own profession a little too much? I mean, what kind of name *is* Mitsui Sonata, anyway?

Not only are you pushing your own ego on me, you even criticise my performances with all these nonsensical complaints. You say things like there's always *something* missing when I play. Every time you open your mouth, it's always about that missing 'something', always going on like a broken record talking about me like I'm such an idiot. I've had enough! I'll never understand what that something is supposed to mean. It's the same with this pamphlet for all these stupid music colleges. You guys love to go on about 'rich musical expression' and 'communicating through sound', but I'm sick of all these meaningless clichés. If music needs a certain something so much, I'd be better off going to a liberal arts university and studying psychology. I've had it with all these stupid somethings, and I don't want to hear it anymore. I just want to focus on good arrangements, so quit pestering me. If you're going to insist I enrol at a music college, then at least I'll join the music education programme and become a music teacher.

I kept on ranting like this to my dad's four-eyed stare with no response, and when I ran out of things to say, I hung up the call.

Even after I closed the application, I was still reeling from the role I had just played and the improvised lines I had blurted out. With my blood rushing to my head like that, I had come out with some pretty wild remarks, but I wasn't lying when I said I was sick to death of all his endless somethings. I decided to honestly consider the possibility of becoming a middle school music teacher. By that point, I had already crossed teaching at a high school off my list because I thought younger students would be easier to handle. I mean, what sort of person would have the nerve to think she could teach in high school while still a high-school student herself?

I tried picturing the faces of all the other students at the middle school I had attended. Dredging up dim memories of what they all did and talked about, I thought to myself how kids between the ages of twelve and fifteen were practically monkeys. Which meant being a middle school music teacher was all about giving those monkeys a break between their five academic subjects to sing songs and do whatever they wanted. I doubted it was so bad a job that my dad would dig in with his objections. Heck, if I *did* set my sights on becoming a music teacher, maybe I wouldn't have to worry about that elusive something anymore.

And so I enrolled in the education programme at

the music college, obtained my teaching licence, passed the official teaching employment examination, and found myself standing at the front of the classroom as a *bona fide* teacher. However, my initial assessment that I could get away with simply letting those wild monkeys sing a few songs turned out to be only half correct. Yes, during the course of my fifty-minute classes with them, all I had to do was let them sing a few songs, play the alto recorder, and let them listen to music on CDs. I also believed one important duty of a music teacher was not to motivate the students any more than absolutely necessary. Middle school students were already busy in their own way, and most of them would chomp on the bit if they were forced to waste their time with overly complicated subjects that had no bearing on their exams. Which was why I designed my classes in a rather dictatorial manner, passing the time while working on my own composition ideas. It was a much more comfortable life than getting a job in some orchestra through my dad's connections.

The problem was I hadn't anticipated exactly what kind of monkeys I would be dealing with. I never would have imagined they would be even more of a hassle outside of class. And would becoming a music teacher really free me from having to think about those stupid somethings? Life wasn't so simple. Teachers were required to keep those somethings in mind at all times. If the only thing they made me waste my energy on was mopping up their blood stains, I would be in heaven. But sometimes, they would come to me with these ridiculous questions, asking things like 'How can I become a famous artist like Yonezu Kenshi?' or 'I've never played an instrument before, but I want to start a band, so can I register a new club with you as our official advisor?' Every year, more such monkeys reared their heads. One and all, they saw music as a fashion trend, an easy way of garnering compliments and attention. But if I didn't handle them properly, their parents would come forward to complain – and once parents were involved, there was no end to a teacher's workload. I had seen colleagues driven to depression and mental illness, ultimately quitting altogether because of the insane pressure put on them by these monkey parent-and-child duos. If someone had earnestly asked me why I wanted to become a music teacher of all things, if they had actually tried to make me reconsider my career path back in high school, maybe everything would have worked out differently.

Shortly after midnight, I received a message from Sae: 'Can you talk over Zoom?' It was the busiest time of year, with just a week to go before the choir festival. I was at home, trying to finish a pile of paperwork, but I decided to join Sae's Zoom call. She was on a business trip to Los Angeles, and before that, she had been in Shanghai or Hong Kong – I wasn't sure which one. It dawned on me that we hadn't spoken for more than a month, not since that conversation about the *Mona Lisa*.

'Sorry. It must be late over there, right?' she asked on the computer screen.

There had been a world of change in internet technology since that Skype call with my dad ten years ago, and the audio quality over Zoom was perfectly clear – which was how I knew, even with the camera switched off, that Sae had been crying.

'There's something I wanted to ask you…' she began, the microphone easily picking up the nasal quality to her voice. 'I won't tell anyone, and no matter what you say, I promise I won't hate you, so please answer me truthfully.'

'Alright.'

I closed my eyes, listening carefully to the sound of her voice over my headphones. Melancholy and nasal though it was, it was reassuring to hear a friend speak when I was stressed and overwhelmed with work.

'I won't beat around the bush. Have you ever done drugs? Illegal ones, like marijuana or that kind of thing?'

'Huh? Did you go to a weed party in LA or something?'

Before I knew it, I was imagining my housemate enjoying herself on the other side of the Pacific Ocean. I was so jealous I found myself clutching my head in frustration.

'And here I am working my arse off to finish the programme in time for this shitty choir festival. Damn it. Maybe I should give up teaching and become an artist myself?'

'No, I didn't do it,' Sae answered, calmly denying the charge. 'Don't get the wrong idea. I know my paintings all look like drunken abstracts to you, but I'm still doing honest work. Anyway, you have, haven't you?'

'No.'

Bothered by the confidence with which she asked that question, I switched my screen from the Zoom call back to my PowerPoint presentation and went back to typing.

Class 1A: Ode to the Earth

Conductor: Nakai Aoi

Accompaniment: Yokota Kanon

'With boundless gratitude toward Mother Earth, the class sings together unified in spirit.'

...

'You mean it? You haven't?' Sae asked, still sceptical.

'You really think I'm high all the time?'

'Sometimes.'

'When?'

'You know, sometimes you stay up three days straight making music. When you get really absorbed in it, you even forget to eat.'

'That's just a natural high. I've been that way ever since I was a kid. It's got nothing to do with drugs.'

'You don't go to clubs or anything?'

'Never. Friends ask me to go with them every now and then, but it's bad for your ears.'

'Your ears?'

'Yeah. Clubs play music at super-loud volumes, right? I don't want to damage my ears, so I don't go to places like that. Right, speaking of clubs...' I said, suddenly remembering the oversized package that had recently arrived in the post. 'My new turntable finally arrived the other day. I didn't have anywhere to put it, so I've left it in your room. It's a good one. Expensive, too.'

I had purchased the scratch turntable at an online auction for use in the last act of the choir festival.

Every year at the choir festival, ten minutes were set aside for a 'Special Performance from the Music Department'. It had become a tradition of sorts for the music teacher to give their own performance at the choir festival, and since there was no real reason not to, I decided to include it again in this year's programme. No teacher before me, however, had put as much time, money, or effort into this special performance as I did. No doubt the first music teacher who started this custom had simply played an amateur ditty on his acoustic guitar to satisfy his own ego – but I, naturally, had no intention of wasting this once-in-a-year opportunity on such a farce.

For my special performances, I liked to set the programme six months in advance, and if necessary, I would spend money of my own to source authentic instruments, even if it meant getting them from overseas. I practiced for at least two hours every day, striving to reach a level of proficiency that I would be proud showing off out there on the stage. I had played the theremin during my first year as a teacher, then the Balinese *gamelan* the second time, the Indian *tabla* the third year, and the *jinghu*, used in Peking Opera, complete with lyrics in Chinese, for my fourth performance. One of the students had uploaded a video of my *gamelan* performance to the internet without my permission, titling it *Music Teacher Gives It Her All During Choir Festival*, and it is still racking up views to this day. Meanwhile, Sae continued to fume about how all these instruments kept up taking up more and more space at home with each passing year.

This year, for my fifth special performance, I had decided to become a DJ. However, that alone, I felt, wasn't quite enough, so I would also be MCing by myself. After all, five years was a milestone, and there was no room for half-measures. For some time now, I had been practicing scratching, refining my lyrics, and studying the kind of flow used in hip-hop, ingraining the tracks into my body. Perhaps part of the reason I was putting so much effort into this ten-minute performance was to offset my lack of passion in my daily lessons. By performing a lesser-known musical genre that my students were unlikely to experience in their everyday lives, I hoped to make up for a year's worth of half-hearted education.

I switched on the camera on the computer and performed a finished portion of the rap to Sae. The title was *Black Monkey*, with black referring to the colour of the students' uniforms. I had been mulling over the lyrics nonstop these past few months, refining and improving on them until I had a strong work with a powerful message.

'Woah. You're performing *that* at the choir festival? You're insane. You could get yourself fired,' Sae exclaimed once I was finished.

Judging from her reaction, the rap had hit all the right notes. I breathed a sigh of relief. Hip-hop was a lot more complicated than it might appear at first glance, and I had struggled to strike the right balance between cool and lame. So long as I was able to convey a sense of edginess to the point where I risked losing my job, then I had embodied the spirit of hip-hop – at least to a small extent.

'It's awesome. I'm at a loss for words,' Sae breathed, deeply moved. 'I can't imagine leaving the house early in the morning to teach music Monday through Friday, and then to make your own music while completely drug-free. You're incredible. You know, I think I get it now. Wouldn't it be great if everyone was like you? If all of humanity thought the same way you do, there would be world peace… No more nuclear weapons…

No more climate change…'

She kept on going, growing increasingly emotional until she was crying to herself nonstop. For the life of me, I couldn't see why *Black Monkey* might have brought her to tears, but I decided not to dwell on that question and continued with my choir festival planning. There was no way to really know what anyone else was thinking, so it was pointless guessing. No matter how hard I tried, I couldn't see the connection between my composing music and the battle against global warming. Wherever you went, folks tried to imagine and empathise with other people's emotions, caught up in the illusion that everyone's hearts and minds were made up of the same materials and worked in the same way. For instance, if I accidentally slipped up and said, 'I don't really like Studio Ghibli movies,' they would respond, 'No way. I don't believe you. Do you even have a human heart?' What they should have been saying was, 'Your heart is different to mine.' So like Sae said, if everyone was like me, if they weren't all arrogantly trying to imagine what went on in other people's heads, maybe there really could be a chance for world peace.

'So what was all that talk of drugs about? I asked when her sobs started growing fewer and farther between, trying to change the subject.

There came a loud clank, as if a chair had been moved, then a long span of silence. Finally, I heard her return to her seat in front of the computer.

'Have you heard of a painter here in LA called Anton?' she asked. 'He's famous for his depictions of animals, but he's also heavily involved in animal rights and environmental issues. He and his wife have adopted three children, and...'

In the middle of this long explanation, I silently removed my headphones, slipped into the kitchen to grab a bottle of wine from the fridge, and then rejoined the call.

'...You see?'

'Yeah.'

'But putting his background aside, I've been a fan of his work for ages, and I was really looking forward to meeting him in person here. We ended up drinking together at his house, and that was when he started smoking marijuana. I've seen plenty of junkie artists in this industry, so I probably shouldn't have been surprised, but it still came as a huge shock, seeing how much I respected him. He asked me to join him, but I turned him down. He didn't act like he minded all that much, but he did say something like it was marijuana that made him the artist he is today, so he's got to be grateful to it. He meant it, too – I could see it in his face.

Then again, he's the kind of person who's thankful for just about anything, not just marijuana – paint, oxygen, even a stain on his shirt. Just look at his Instagram account if you want to know what I mean. In pretty much all his posts, he's saying thank you for something.'

'Huh.'

'Anyway, the marijuana must have loosened his lips, because after that, he became real chatty, showing me pictures of his works before and after he started taking drugs and explaining all the differences. And I mean, there *was* a huge difference between them. The ones he did after taking marijuana were inspired by his hallucinations, and they were soul-crushingly better. There was a real sense of direction in them, a real strength to the lines. It was like I could see into his soul with his choice of colour. And then I started to lose track of everything… Basically, the works I found so moving – they were all products of his drug-fuelled hallucinations. Talk about stupid, right? They weren't even proper art. The *purity* of art is completely lost once drugs are brought into the equation… But then again, people say you should always separate the artist from the artwork, right? Right?'

'Er… I suppose so.'

I stopped playing with the mouse to try to digest everything she was saying. Marijuana. Hallucinations.

Purity… I thought about changing the topic to jazz music seeing as I knew next to nothing about paintings, but I stopped myself when I realised that probably wasn't the point of this call.

The silence stretched out between us. There wasn't anything wrong with the Wi-Fi connection – Sae was simply waiting for me to express a meaningful opinion.

At last –

'Right, yeah. People do need to separate the artist from their work,' I said. 'Even someone like Van Gogh – I mean, wouldn't he be super offended if he knew how everyone pities him today, how people associate his tragic life with his work all the time?'

I honestly didn't care about some nineteenth-century Dutch maniac who cut off his own ear, but it was the best comparison I could come up with on the spot. It seemed to strike a chord, though, as Sae broke into a fit of even more forceful sobs. 'I know, right? It's just like Van Gogh.' I took my headphones off there and turned the computer volume down to its lowest level.

I heard her blow her nose several times, then get up from her seat to get something to eat or drink. Neither of us said anything for the longest time, but as I breathed in the various sounds of everyday life, my thoughts turned to Sae. She had achieved considerable success as a painter, to the point she was probably the envy of most of her peers, but she still tried to confront what art meant in an abstract sense, wrestled with what it was supposed to be. Faced with her artistic earnestness – or rather, her fastidiousness – I felt a little guilty for my earlier remark about giving up teaching and becoming an artist myself.

Once she had regained her composure somewhat –

'Hey, I'm sorry. Can you stay on the line a little longer?' she asked politely.

'What's the matter?'

'You switched your camera on when you were rapping earlier, you know?'

'Yeah.'

'It's been on this whole time. I can see your face.'

'Huh. So it is.'

On checking, it seemed I had indeed left the camera on. I had wanted to show her my hand movements while rapping, but I didn't need it anymore, so I switched it off.

'I've stopped it.'

'Um, you don't have to turn it off, not if you don't want to.'

'Hmm?'

'Look, I'm not accusing you of anything,' she said awkwardly. 'I just wanted to ask you, um… You knew

I was crying just now, right? You can tell I'm overcome with grief here, yeah?'

'Huh? Sure.'

'It's not like I expect you to feel sad just because I am. I get it. But, er… I need to know. Why were you smiling to yourself while I was crying? You had a huge grin on your face, didn't you? You were on the camera for a full five minutes. So I'm just wondering why you look so happy?'

'Ah.'

I finally understood what she was trying to say. Clenching my fists, I gently massaged my cheeks with my knuckles, hoping to loosen the muscles.

'Didn't I tell you? I've started doing facial muscle training. I've been doing it at home, pretty much unconsciously. I wasn't laughing because you're crying or anything. I'm just working on my face muscles. So don't sweat it.'

'Ah… Right, I see. Facial muscles… No, I *don't* really get it… But alright. Whatever, I don't care. I don't care, alright? I'm sorry.'

Personally, I didn't mind her seeing me while practicing my face exercises, but she seemed to think the situation incredibly awkward.

Maybe she thought she was being discreet, but for whatever reason, she abruptly changed the subject.

'By the way,' she began as she started going on about a French movie called *Blue is the Warmest Colour*. Apparently, she watched it on Netflix while staying at her hotel.

'So there's this schoolteacher, Adèle, and her older live-in girlfriend, Emma, who's a painter. Hey, doesn't this setup sound a bit like us? We might not be lovers, but we're a teacher and a painter living together. Anyway, they're both women, and they fall madly in love. But the longer they live together, the more things keep going wrong. The painter is played by Léa Seydoux. Do you know her?'

'Nope,' I answered. Sae went on to list several more names and proper nouns from various fields, but they all flew right over my head. Then again, I struggled to even remember my own students' names.

'You should try showing an interest in something other than music for a change,' Sae went on. 'Anyway, the film's R-rated, and it's got some really extensive sex scenes with the two main characters. They're super explicit, with close-ups showing basically every pore of their skin. They're so graphic they make you feel like you've got heartburn watching them. I'll be honest with you, I don't really like sex scenes. I don't want to be seen as narrow-minded as an artist, but I just haven't worked out my own thoughts on how sex can be elevated to the domain of art… Anyway, I was watching those endless sex scenes, wondering when they were finally going to end, when I started feeling all out of breath. I'd had enough, seriously – I just wanted it to stop. That scene was supposed to be the moment you feel the intensity of the love that exists between the two main characters, but all I felt was discomfort. All these unnecessary thoughts started flooding through my mind, and I couldn't help but ask myself if Léa Seydoux really wanted to perform these long sex scenes for the sake of art. Basically, I wasn't thinking about the character Emma in the movie, but the actress working naked, surrounded by a huge crew, with all these lights and cameras pointed her way. In the end, I couldn't understand why the film needed such long sex scenes – it just left me feeling exhausted… Of course, I know Léa Seydoux is a top-notch actress, the kind who approaches every scene with a strong sense of professionalism. But I was curious, so I did some research on the movie. And I found an article where Léa Seydoux said how painful those scenes were to shoot for her. She mentioned being constantly pressured by the director, a man called Kechiche, to do the scenes, and all they did was fill her with anxiety. She went so far as to say she never wants to work with him again. So, in the end, a film completed only by putting a woman through all this mental anguish got massive critical acclaim and even ended up getting the Palme d'Or at Cannes. But if you ask me, it would have been better if they'd never made the thing in the first place. I don't trust art made by some asshole who can't even bring himself to imagine a woman's pain. People like that are imposters, fakes, and…'

There was no end to Sae's long diatribe, and so –

'Hold on,' I interrupted. 'Didn't you say you like my music?'

'Yes, I like it,' she replied without hesitation.

'But what if, hypothetically, I was, like, a super-bad person? Would you lose faith in my music?'

'What? I don't see how that's possible,' she said, caught by surprise. 'I already know you're a good person… Sure, you're easily misunderstood, and you won't even clean your own room – but living with you, I know you're pure at heart. And that purity is reflected in your music, so – '

'You say I'm pure, but I've done a lot of bad stuff over the years, you know? Not as extreme as abusing marijuana or forcing someone like Léa Seydoux to do sex scenes, but every now and then, I've committed small sins of my own.'

'Like what?'

I turned my mind to one of my most recent guilty

pleasures, a story I had planned to take to the grave. It was the kind of thing I couldn't divulge to my colleagues no matter what, even if it killed me. But I couldn't think of anything else more appropriate to make my point. And so, with my brain still unsure whether I should really go through with it, I said: 'You know those matching apps, right? I've been using one for the past month or so to scout for guys.'

'You're kidding, right?' Sae said, her voice increasing in volume.

'Nope. I lied about my age when I signed up. I'm on the lookout for young college-aged guys who've just moved to Tōkyō.'

'Woah. That *is* pretty bad.'

Though she seemed slightly taken aback, her reaction was more one of curiosity and amusement. I couldn't see her, but it didn't take much imagination to picture her leaning forward with a grin, waiting on my every word as they reverberated through her headphones.

'I don't mean to be rude, but to be honest, it's a bit of a relief to hear you actually have normal human desires. I guess what I'm feeling is reassurance…?'

'Huh? Normal human desires?'

'Well, let's put that aside for now. So, what happened?' Sae asked, urging me to continue.

'So, those matching apps are just filled with desperate guys chasing after sex, right? It's pretty easy to get a match right away, and if you want, you can meet them that very night. The trick is to go for guys who have insecurities about their height. Guys like that are never popular, so if you say something like "I really love short guys, they're so cute" or whatever, you can reel them in in one shot.'

'You *are* bad,' Sae coughed, chortling with laughter. 'You're an evil, wicked teacher. When I get back to Japan, I'm totally reporting you.'

Emboldened by her response, I couldn't stop myself from wanting to up the ante.

'So, if you do that, you can set up a date with some young, fresh-skinned, short, preferably baby-faced lightweight guy. Then, while eating dinner with him, you can try to get a feel for how compatible you are. If he's the kind who listens to whatever you have to say, he's perfect. I like them easy-going, the kind who isn't too self-conscious. If I get the impression it isn't going to work out, I'll just have dinner and leave. But if I think we've got chemistry, we'll go to a hotel. And what do you think we do there?'

'Huh? You have sex, right?'

'Yeah, sure, but that isn't really the point. It wouldn't really bother me if we skipped it altogether. What matters is this – I tell the guy I've brought with me he has to address me like his teacher.'

'Hah?'

'And not just any teacher – I make him play the role of a middle school student. I've basically got a whole script ready to go. Want to hear it? "I'm such an idiot, Ms Mitsui. I'm a middle school student who fell in love with a classmate, punched my friend, and forgot to practice the alto recorder. I'm sorry for always causing you so much trouble." That's what I make him say, then I tell him to kowtow on the bed to apologise. And I say to him: "You really are a naughty student. But don't worry – I'll discipline you until you change your attitude and learn to focus on your studies. You're always such a headache, but if you can please me, I'll be willing to forgive you". And then I make him say – '

'Huh? Don't tell me you're being serious?' Sae interrupted in a low voice.

She had been so excited to hear this story just a brief moment ago, but now her words dripped with undisguised disgust and contempt. I had had some inkling this might happen, and sure enough, her moral compass simply couldn't tolerate this tale. Over the years, I had witnessed plenty of variations of her emotional displays, but never before had I felt the sheer intensity of anger that now leaked out from my headphones. In most situations that would rile people's anger, Sae was the kind of person who turned first to sadness. Instead of feeling anger toward despicable individuals, for instance, she would mourn the society that had created them. This time, however, her indignation was directed straight at me, personally, devoid of her usual meta viewpoint or cushion of pity.

'I'm not saying I actually want to have sex with middle school students,' I added hastily. 'I don't think about my students that way. It's just a game…' But try as I might to set the record straight, it was already too late.

'You're disgusting. You're a fucking psycho teacher,' Sae spat as she ended the call.

The room had already been practically silent until Sae called, but now that her voice had cut out, I couldn't bear it anymore. Closing my laptop, I exhaled deeply to release the tension that had built up in my chest and leaned back in my work chair. While staring up at the ceiling, I noticed an accordion lying shrivelled up on the bookshelf. I decided to rescue the poor instrument, tiptoeing around and clearing the clutter standing in my path. Then, putting the straps over my shoulders and holding the accordion against my body to play it for the first time in years, a familiar sound resonated throughout the room, just as I remembered. It was like the voice of a huge, ugly man. With each note, clouds of white dust that had accumulated on the bellows were sent dancing through the air. Coughing as I inhaled the dust, I set about playing the entirety of The Beatles' *White Album* from start to finish. Yet when I tried playing *The Continuing Story of Bungalow Bill*, my fingering went haywire, throwing my tempo off, and no matter how many times I tried, I just couldn't get a satisfactory take. That was when I realised I was unmistakably pissed off at Sae.

Even after listening to my story and calling me 'a fucking psycho teacher', she still hadn't told me if her perspective on my music had changed. I felt inclined to rip into her for abruptly ending the call without answering the most important question. Since when did she become so selfish? She was already getting on in years, and yet she went about sobbing, laughing, and blowing a fuse. She was mentally unstable, overly sensitive, the Reiwa era's very own Ono Yōko.

After thoroughly chewing her out to an audience of zero, my chest started to ache for real this time. It was a weird pain, like the organs surrounding my heart were expanding and compressing all at once, and it made me think of the time I first met Sae. She had been crying then, too, and we had talked about music and art.

No. Hold on.

It wasn't Sae I talked about music and art with. I forget his name, but it was another painter, a man.

I was visiting an art college in Tōkyō as a performer for an event. Basically, it was a part-time job – I would play the piano a little while some art student gave a painting performance. Back in my college days, friends and acquaintances would introduce me to all sorts of music-related jobs, and at the time, I needed money to buy equipment for composing music and to visit the Blue Note, so I accepted every little thing that came my way.

A few days before the event, I was introduced to the painter at a sort of pre-meeting. He was a creepy guy, with a strange habit of staring back at you through overly wide eyes between gaps in his long fringe. I hadn't slept much that night, so I was groggy the whole day. During the meeting, the people from the art college kept throwing about all these artistic terms I'd never heard before, only adding to my confusion, and to make matters worse, the performance had some ridiculous title like *Music and Painting for Musical Painting and Painterly Music*. By that point, my mood was already going into a tailspin.

The man told me he liked to base his artworks on images gleaned from music. On the day of the event, he would be using a painting already ninety percent complete as his base, and I would play live music to inspire him to add the finishing touches.

'So, Mitsui, I want you to express the feelings you get from my performance in sound,' he said, staring into my eyes.

His unwavering confidence that his painting would arouse a sense of musical creativity in his performer was frankly unsettling. I was just a college student, and I felt like I had taken on an impossible job. Sure, my parents had dragged me along to art museums and the like ever since I was a kid as part of my so-called 'cultural education', but I had never had any real opinions about the works, let alone likes and dislikes. If I had to rate any painting on a five-point scale, I would never give a score other than three. My impressions were neither here nor there.

Once we had gone over the arrangements for the day, the man seemed overly eager to hear about my personal life. He was particularly insistent about my dad. 'How has he influenced you? What does he think of your playing style?'

And so, to that ridiculously uptight question, I answered: 'If you knew all about me in advance, wouldn't those non-musical elements influence your work on the day?'

Naturally, I wasn't being sarcastic. He kept repeating the words 'pure musical experience' again and again throughout his explanation, so I genuinely thought any personal information might end up blemishing the spontaneity of the event. In retrospect, I probably didn't need to worry so much about his artistry. All he wanted was to add a little substance to our bio, which read simply: 'Working together with Mitsui Sonata, daughter of the famed Mitsui Yōji, and currently a highly acclaimed student studying in music college.'

Despite several misgivings, I managed to finish the job, troublesome though it was. Recognising flowers in his painting, I decided to play songs with flowery titles one after another, from Lange's *Blumenlied* to Schubert's *Heidenröslein* to *Flower* by Taki Rentarō to Tchaikovsky's *Snowdrop*. When I ran out of flower-related songs, I started improvising with romantic music. Overall, the audience seemed generally satisfied.

Unfortunately, I didn't take away any *impressions* from the painter's performance. There was one song

I felt an overpowering urge to play while watching him at his craft, however – Liszt's *Totentanz*. This was because I couldn't feel any impact that my performance was having on the man's painting. I felt like all I was doing was adding background music to a pre-existing artwork. This wasn't a collaboration between music and painting – it wasn't anything. But since the event was supposedly all about our inspiring each other, I wanted to see if I could express my music in lines and colours. And if the man really could take something away from my music, then it was possible the heavy dissonance that characterised the *Totentanz* could darken the flowers. If I did that, maybe even I, tone-deaf to painting, would be able to realise the meaning of the word 'collaboration'. Yes, rather than trying to achieve a predictable harmony, what I had been waiting for, without even fully realising it, was a dramatic rebirth.

But in the end, I didn't have the courage to play the Liszt piece, sticking to a loose selection that was neither too colourful nor too dull until the event came to a close. As for the finished painting, I had no real opinion on it. All the same, I did feel a sense of accomplishment thanks to the unparalleled sounds resonating from the piano. It was just a plain old Yamaha C Series, but maybe because of the shape of the hall, it sounded infinitely better than most ordinary pianos – less like the notes were simply vibrations passing through the air to reach my ears, and more like the cells inside my eardrums had literally morphed into waves of pure sound. Even after the audience broke into a round of applause and the painter left surrounded by his entourage, I still couldn't bring myself to leave the piano. I could have played on for a full ten hours. Heck, if I played every song I wanted to hear with those crisp, mellow notes, it would easily have exceeded ten hours.

I did eventually get up from my seat, only to have a change of heart and turn to a nearby staff member to ask if I could keep on playing. The woman seemed puzzled for a moment, but when I subtly dropped my dad's name, she allowed me to stay (I had a bad habit of using my dad's name for personal benefit about once a year). Then, free from all restrictions, I played all the songs that came to mind. Mozart. Bill Evans. Piazzolla. Burt Bacharach. João Gilberto. Michel Legrand. Chick Corea. James Brown. Stevie Wonder. Radiohead.

No matter which one I played, the abnormal sounds continued to reverberate. None of the staff members, however, were left shaken by this situation, proceeding to clean up the venue in stoic silence. I was in such a bizarre state of agitation that I couldn't help but wonder whether some strange substance had been slipped into the jasmine tea the staff prepared for me. Though I didn't realise it at the time, I had already fallen into that distinct sense of *drunkenness.* Engrossed by the sounds of the piano, I experienced a nonsensical hallucination where frozen sardines were sticking vertically out of my head while hot tofu miso soup sizzled and gushed from the wounds. Soaking in that pool of miso soup, I felt my bladder relaxing – and only barely stopped myself from wetting my pants. It was while walking this dangerous tightrope that a score by Rachmaninoff popped out of nowhere and landed in my hands.

I knew for a fact that if I had an accident in a place like this, it would haunt me for the rest of my days. There were still more than a few staff members lingering in the hall. And yet I couldn't resist my own curiosity. What would happen if I played the Rachmaninoff piece on this piano? It didn't make any sense, passing on Rachmaninoff because of mere bodily fluids. After all, if I couldn't hold it in, all I had to so was mop it up afterward. I knew perfectly well how to remove stains.

Once I had finished playing Pharrell Williams's latest song, I paused to take a deep breath, loosened my belt to relieve the pressure on my bladder, and removed my jacket, damp with sweat, hanging it on the back of my chair. At that moment, my eyes made contact with those of a woman standing directly behind me. It was Sae, back then still a student at the art college. She stood there, wiping tears from her bloodshot eyes with the back of her hand.

'Um, are you okay?' I called out unknowingly, caught off guard by her unusual appearance.

'I'm sorry,' she answered with a pained look. 'That song you just played, I think it struck a chord in my heart… I've never been so moved by music before… Um, your name is Mitsui Sonata, right?'

In her hand, she was clutching a pamphlet for the collaborative event, complete with my name emblazoned on the front.

'Ah,' I sighed, neither a true answer nor a proper exhale, placing the cover over the piano keys and lowering the lid.

As soon as I saw those tears, my head and body, both so heated just a moment ago, rapidly cooled. I even had the composure to ask myself whether I had been touched by the music or if I had just experienced one of those so-called 'soul-stirring' moments. My mind was perfectly clear. Gone was my obsession with Rachmaninoff and everything else. In fact, I felt like punching myself for trying to go ahead with a public performance when I was on the cusp of wetting my pants.

The woman – Sae – however, pressed both hands up against her chest, that movement all but declaring she was positively filled with emotion. 'That's a really wonderful name, Sonata. It's like you were born to play the piano.'

'Stop. Please, stop. It's embarrassing,' I said, thrusting my hands in front of me in a gesture of restraint. 'Seriously, I'm not Princess Mononoke or anything. Cut it out.'

'Princess Mononoke?'

'I mean it, don't call me that, please. And I wasn't born to play the piano. Seriously, it doesn't make any sense. You don't have any consciousness before you're born. So I was born first, then given the name, and I only decided to play piano after that.'

In the end, I didn't catch so much as a wink of shut-eye. I played *White Album* to its conclusion, then got dressed when it was time for me to leave the house and headed to work. After a whole morning packed full of lessons, I was too exhausted to eat a leisurely lunch in the classroom. When fourth period rolled around, I pilfered a carton of milk from the classroom and headed straight for the music prep room. There, I threw my yoga mat, which I used for meditating, on the floor, lay down on it, slammed my headphones on, and selected my Satie playlist. The sound of Sae's voice still rang fresh in my ears, and I wanted to rid myself of this tightness in my chest as quickly as possible. But even after ten rounds of the *Gymnopédies*, those last words she uttered before disconnecting the Zoom call wouldn't leave me in peace.

Disconnecting the useless Satie, I turned to my iPhone. Tears were the best medicine at times like this. And so, clinging to that overly simplistic hope, I typed the words 'touching, emotional music' into the search bar in YouTube and started playing the top-ranking videos one by one. Those songs, however, with titles like *Tearjerkers* and *Guaranteed to Make You Cry*, had no physical effect on me whatsoever. Had my tear ducts atrophied, losing the ability to produce tears altogether?

Come to think of it, I couldn't remember shedding a single tear since the day Michael Jackson died more than ten years ago. With that recollection, I closed the YouTube app with its not-quite tearjerking music and went back to my playlist, searching for *Dirty Diana*. I felt for sure I would be able to bawl my eyes out to the sound of Michael Jackson shouting 'Dirty Diana!'

It felt like the perfect choice for the occasion, but even that failed. Just as the song was building up to its chorus and I was getting caught in the mood, it was cut short by a dry knocking at the door.

It was no regular knock. No, it was much more confident than that, as if the person on the other side knew I was in here. But that didn't make any sense. The music prep room was upholstered with a seamless fabric so no one could see in from outside. Not a soul in the school ought to have known I was holed up in this cramped, dusty space, a graveyard for disused instruments.

Since the door was locked anyway, I held my breath, trying to pretend I wasn't home. Whoever it was, though, knocked a second, then a third time, until –

'Ms Mitsui Sonata,' sounded a voice calling out my name.

Resigned to my fate, I put my headphones down and opened the door, staring across at the face of the female student waiting for me there.

'Yokota Kanon,' I said, naming her in turn.

You might say that out of all my current students, she was the one I had the most interactions with. Not only was she in my homeroom class, she was also a member of the music department and of the brass band club I was responsible for supervising. On top of that, she would be playing the piano at the upcoming choir festival. She had an incredibly serious attitude toward classwork, boasted excellent grades, and never broke the school's dress code. Maybe it was her parents' influence, but she always tied her bangs back with an old-fashioned hairband and used polite language with her teachers. Her handwriting was obsessively perfect, to the extent I had to be a little careful with my own scribble when marking up her papers in red pen.

Apart from our relationship as teacher and student, there was also a personal interaction I had had with her that left an unusually strong impression. It happened one class just before summer vacation. Unlike most students who saw their afternoon music lessons as an extension of lunch break, Yokota was highly attentive, taking notes all throughout, as was her usual wont. That day, I spent the majority of the fifty-minute class giving a one-sided lecture on the establishment and history of opera, and in the last three minutes, I showed a video of Luciano Pavarotti singing *Nessun Dorma* on the projector screen. Watching the clip, Yokota was so engrossed in the video she didn't even blink, shedding such a deluge of tears that I could see them even from the lectern at the front of the room. I had played this video numerous times during my five years as a teacher, but never before had anyone reacted even remotely like this.

Apparently, she wanted to talk about the choir festival, so I locked the door to the prep room and led her into the music room. Once inside, I closed the door behind me and asked her to continue.

'I want us to aim for the gold medal,' she said.

For a moment, I wondered what on earth she was talking about – but then I realised she was saying she wanted Class 1A to win the top prize at the upcoming choir festival.

However, to cut a long story short, that was an impossible proposition. To begin with, the faculty had already decided the gold medal would go to a third-year class, the silver one to a second-year class, and the bronze one to a first-year class. In all the years of the choir festival, this tradition had never once been overturned – as, indeed, anyone would know if they looked over the records of previous events. I was more than a little surprised to see Yokota, who usually picked up on these things fairly quickly, acting like any other clueless student. She seemed to genuinely believe the festival was judged purely on merit, that a first-year student actually had a real chance of winning first place depending on how well they performed.

She was peering straight into my eyes. Even after all these years, I still wasn't comfortable looking these children in the eye, so I quickly shifted my gaze upward. I couldn't help but notice the soft, downy hairs that didn't quite fit in her headband falling on her pale forehead in gentle waves.

'I don't want to come off as rude, but…' She closed her eyes for a second with a troubled look, a deep vertical line emerging between her eyebrows. Somehow, it gave her a remarkably dignified air. 'I'll be playing the piano, which means I won't be doing any singing myself. So I feel like I can give an objective assessment of the chorus. As things stand, I don't think our class can win the gold medal – or silver or bronze, for that matter. We could even end up losing to Class 1B. But I can't just sit by in silence while we're floundering so badly. I absolutely do *not* want us to put in a bad showing, especially seeing as you're our homeroom teacher, Ms Mitsui. We only have six more days before the performance, and excluding the weekend, just four days left to practice. But I'm determined to turn our chances around, no matter what.'

She spoke in a hurry, without the polished composure she normally maintained throughout class. For the life of me, I just couldn't understand why she was so fixated on winning. There was nothing wrong with showing a little enthusiasm for school events, but she had never been that type of student before. Was she already looking ahead to her high-school applications, worrying about her internal exam scores?

'Please, be honest with me, Ms Mitsui. What do you think about our class's performance?' She stared back at me with a stern look, like a scientist observing a tiny bug under a microscope, trying not to miss even the smallest change.

'I think they're getting better,' I answered unflinchingly. And it wasn't a lie. 'Especially over the past few days. The girls have found their voices, and they're making fewer pitch mistakes. It might be a little difficult for a first-year class to win the gold medal, though, seeing as it's your first choir festival and there are more experienced students in higher grades. But if we aim for the bronze prize, it's definitely within reach,'

I said encouragingly, hoping she would catch my drift. With that, I tugged at my facial muscles to flash her the strongest smile I could muster.

By now, I was confident I could handle almost any facial expression, even in unexpected situations without a mirror. I knew from long practice how to position my muscles and the folds of my skin. The face I hoped to wear right now was that of a teacher trusting in the infinite potential of her students.

Yokota, however, wore an increasingly gloomy look, her ears turning bright red. 'But Ms Mitsui, you're always telling us to focus on our diaphragms, to open our mouths wide and sing from the bottom of our stomachs... Personally, I don't think that's a great method. I should have said something earlier, but just singing loudly doesn't make good music. If all it takes is yelling, even monkeys could do it. But we're not monkeys.'

'Of course not. You aren't monkeys,' I said, the words leaving my mouth a stark contrast to the thoughts occupying my head. I had to turn my attention to the muscles between my eyebrows and at the corners of my mouth to maintain my next expression.

Naturally, I had overseen every class's chorus rehearsals, and there honestly wasn't much difference between Class 1A and Class 1B. When I said Yokota's class had a real chance of taking the third-place prize, I meant it. But if she felt her classmates' singing was inferior to Class 1B, the reason no doubt lay solely with the three fatally tone-deaf boys who by a stroke of ill fortune had all been assigned to Class 1A. Their powerful vocal cords produced the most discordant singing, throwing the other students off and making them fall out of rhythm. If I wanted to dramatically improve the situation, the quickest way would be to give the three of them detention to provide them with some one-on-one training – but not only would that be grossly unfair, it would no doubt wound their pride. For a generation that had grown up with karaoke and sing-along videos, tone deafness was a very sensitive issue. So as a compromise, I had been working on improving the other students' volume, though the process was certainly taking a fair amount of time. If the overall volume went up, the voices of those three tone-deaf boys would be harder for the audience to make out. And so I *had* made a concerted effort to help the students improve their singing, and the chorus had improved dramatically as a result. It seemed Yokota, however, didn't quite appreciate my instruction. She may have had enough musical sensitivity to cry her eyes out to Pavarotti, but she had a poor ear.

'You don't seem to have good hearing. What would someone like you know about music?' I felt like saying, but I wrestled that urge to the ground, maintaining my smile in an effort to soothe her anxiety and impatience. I was in perfect control. It was a shame no one else was around to witness the fruit of my daily training. I glanced over at the window in the door, hoping against hope that someone might have thought to check in on us. After all, anyone looking on would surely think to themselves: 'Wow, Ms Mitsui's such a great teacher.' They would think I had boundless empathy for my students. There was no way they could call me a bad teacher.

Clenching her teeth, Yokota stared down at her feet for a full minute or so as if to hold back tears, until –

'I've been wondering something since the start of the school year. I know this is rude, Ms Mitsui, but do you mind?' she asked hesitantly.

'Not at all. Go ahead,' I replied with a gentle smile.

'First, I thought I was just uncomfortable. But lately, all these things have been piling up, and I'm starting to lose faith in you… Um, your father is Mitsui Yōji, the musician, right? I don't think many people at school have heard of him.'

'Indeed, that's right. You're very astute, Miss Yokota. Not many young people these days recognise my father's name.'

I incorporated a hint of approachability into my soft smile. It was easy. After all, I was genuinely amused she thought I might feel flustered by such a trivial question.

Nonetheless, what she said next most definitely did leave me shaken.

'Music is all about a love of sound, right? That's how it's written in Japanese, with the characters for "sound" and "enjoyment", right? But I don't get the feeling you really *do* enjoy it, Ms Mitsui. The way you approach music...it's like something's missing. At first, I thought I was just imagining things, but now, I'm sure... Actually, I've been dating a boy in second year, and he told me about something that happened recently. Back in September, he got injured here in the music room, and he said you took him to the infirmary. But apparently, you weren't worried at all about his injury... Is it true? Not only were you not worried about it, he said he heard you snickering as you stood over him. He said you sounded annoyed. That made me really sad, hearing that. Frankly, I thought right then you must be a lousy teacher. That you don't have a heart. What could someone like that possibly understand about music...?'

I covered my mouth with my left hand, pinching the pit of my stomach with my right one. My abdominal muscles contracted, robbing my upper body of any sense of balance and almost sending me toppling over. If not for the piano behind me, I would have fallen flat on the ground. I was in danger here, I thought. This was more than just a surprise attack. Heck, this rebuke was genuinely comical. If I let my guard down, I would probably burst out in laughter.

Memories that I had long suppressed came flooding back, and my well-trained facial muscles were rendered utterly useless in the face of the tangled deluge of emotions. I never imagined the individual at the centre of the bloodstain incident would come forward in such a manner, nor that the 'female student' both Omi and Fujiwara stubbornly refused to identify during the subsequent 'discussion' would belong to my own class, and certainly not that she would come forward so easily… Yokota's impeccable sense of timing as she delivered those lines felt like the cruellest of jokes, causing my body to freeze up. My voice was tied back by the muscles around my mouth, and there was nothing I could do to hold back the unbearably hot feeling welling up behind my eyelids.

And there she went, tears already streaming down her face. With a moist, sharp-eyed gaze, she continued to peer into my eyes in anticipation. I struggled to wrap my head around this sudden standoff, desperately racking my brains to unearth the reason for her tears.

Question: Why was Yokota Kanon crying?

1. Because I was a poor excuse for a teacher.

2. Because she felt sorry for Omi, seeing as I wasn't worried about his injury.

3. Because she felt sorry for herself, having enrolled at a school with a terrible music teacher.

4. Because she felt like despairing at the incompetence of Japan's teacher licensing system, allowing even the most despicable individuals to become teachers.

Those four possibilities all came to mind, but I gave up on deciding which was the correct one. This was beyond my expertise. Maybe I would ask the Japanese language teacher when I bumped into her in the staffroom.

By sheer force of will, I succeeded in keeping the tears watering up in my eyes to the bare minimum.

'Right, right,' I said. 'How about this, then?'

Yokota accepted my proposal, so we took a vote during homeroom class just a few hours later. There was no time to engage in any further abstract discussion of music. First, Yokota gave a speech at the front of the room on the current issues facing the class's singing and outlined her plans for the choir. Her argument was the class should move away from its emphasis on volume and shift to a focus on emotional expression. She exhorted her classmates to take the profound message of *Ode to the Earth* to heart and to sing in a way that would resonate with the judges. After her speech, I distributed notepaper to the thirty-two other students (Yokota excluded) and asked them to write the name of the person they thought more suitable to lead them for the remaining four days of choir practice, either me or her. Then, I went to my car to grab my cajón, which I held between my legs during my commute, and had them place their votes within the instrument's sound hole.

I didn't need to open the cajón to know the outcome – there was no way a mere music teacher would be able to compete with a teenage girl who had so effortlessly toyed with the hearts of two older boys in other classes. Yokota's popularity was overwhelming. I understood that from the very beginning, yet seeing it quantified so plainly was beyond disheartening. If I had known things would turn out this way, I would have perhaps given a lecture on composing music in the style of Yonezu Kenshi to increase my likability, seeing how much the students seemed to admire him. Not only did my housemate hate me, now, my own students despised me, too. It was enough to leave me feeling utterly hopeless. I had never once thought of myself as a *good* teacher, but I took pride in the fact I had always done my best with the students. Even if I didn't have what it took to be a truly great teacher, I had put in the training and work to at least come across as halfway decent. Which was why I never would have dreamed I might be treated this way by my own class.

Swept off my feet by the torrent of fast-moving emotions, I lost all confidence in my ability to control my facial expressions. In the staffroom, I pulled a mask from the box I kept at my table. Fitting it over my face felt like a declaration of defeat, but it was all so I could focus my remaining energies on the choir festival. And so I decided to hide my face and put aside all thought of facial muscles until the event was over.

And so Sae's prophecy came true prematurely, as I was indeed, for all intents and purposes, fired from my role as the class's teacher. From that afternoon onward, Yokota became the choir's instructor, and an entirely new set of lessons was underway.

To begin with, Yokota fixed a picture she had no doubt printed in the audio-visual room to the blackboard, explaining it was a painting by Gauguin called *Delightful Land*. Her reason for sharing the painting with the class seemed to be to nurture a sense of gratitude to the Earth, which was also the central theme of our class's song. I knew a little bit about Gauguin. He probably painted *Delightful Land* while in Tahiti, using a local girl as a model. It was an exotic painting of a solidly-built, healthy-looking girl with a yellowish complexion, standing stark naked. I could easily imagine this artwork attracting complaints from parents, however. After all, the girl's nipples and pubic hair were boldly depicted, and a quick internet search revealed she had only been thirteen years old at the time, which coincidentally was the same age as most of our first-year students. Praying that no passing teachers would spot it up there on the blackboard, I quietly opened my laptop at the back of the room and pretended to busy myself preparing new teaching materials, careful not to make the class's new teacher feel like she was being too closely monitored during rehearsal.

And so, in just four days, the chorus I had spent the past two months building up was thoroughly destroyed. The new teacher even went so far as to praise the off-key singing of the three tone deaf boys, saying: 'That's great, you're really putting your hearts into it.' Her novel teaching method inevitably led to the trio getting more and more carried away, and the chorus became more chaotic by the day. Sounds that anyone would expect in a choir went unheard, while those that shouldn't have existed at all took centre stage. And there I was, fighting an unacknowledged insanity under a mask, cornered by a situation that satisfied both definitions of 'drunkenness'. It went beyond mere intoxication – it was like I was plagued by the nausea and headache of a severe hangover, unable to muster my voice. I scribbled on the blackboard that I had caught a cold and had a sore throat, and until the day of the choir festival itself, I refrained from uttering so much as a word.

The most notable feature of Yokota's *Ode to the Earth* was the climax at the end. A new piece of choreography had been added as the grand finale to her version of the song. Once the carefully and solemnly built-up chorus reached its peaks, the students would raise their hands into the sky as a group and call out: 'Praise the Earth! Oh!'

They would start lifting their hands into the air with the word 'praise', reach their heads with 'Earth', and then turn their faces up to the heavens with the final 'Oh!'. This surprise performance was supposedly intended to 'express our gratitude to the Earth with all our being', a secret plan Yokota had no doubt devised based on foreign movies like *Sister Act* and *Pitch Perfect* or TV shows like *Glee*.

'But if you want to thank the Earth, shouldn't you be prostrating yourselves on the ground, not raising your hands up to the heavens?' I almost blurted out while sneaking a peek over the rim of my glasses at this choreography rehearsal. Thankfully, my mask prevented me from actually speaking out loud, but the moment that insipid piece of advice crossed my mind, I started seriously considering resigning my teaching position for real.

Once the choir festival was done and dusted, I carted the turntable, mixer, and microphone I had used in the performance back home and found Sae freshly returned from her trip to Los Angeles. 'Welcome back,' I called out when I found her busy putting away the contents of her oversized suitcase. 'I'm home,' she answered. Her moods were usually much more straightforward, but at that moment, I couldn't read anything from her profile. Maybe she still hated me, maybe she didn't. Either way, I was exhausted, so I went to take a shower.

After finishing in the bathroom and drying my hair, I opened a bottle of sparkling wine and sank into the couch to watch the news on TV. There didn't seem to be any major national news, as the newscaster was focusing on economic events in America. Sae seated herself next to me, brushing the tips of her hair.

'Was the choir festival today?' she asked.

'Yeah.'

'Did your rap go down well?'

'Yep,' I nodded, switching off the TV. 'You could

probably call it the culmination of my teaching career.'

'That's good to hear.'

'It is. Really good. I made real music. Because that's what music is. You understand what I mean, don't you? I *was* the music.'

'Huh? Right, of course. I get that… Huh? It went well, then? Everyone at the school was happy with it?' Sae wore an anxious frown.

'At the school? What would be the point pleasing *them*? Don't be stupid… Ah, right. You probably haven't heard, seeing as you were in the air at the time. There was a slight mishap during the festival.'

After downing half my mug of wine, I found myself staring absentmindedly at the drug-inspired abstract painting on the wall, my mug still pressed against my lips. The living room was a shambles, all but overflowing with the contents of the souvenir bag Sae had brought back and the rubbish I had left lying about while she was away. I had been so busy preparing for the choir festival I hadn't even run the washing machine in over a week. And when was the last time I did any dishes? I thought about putting some background music on to take my mind off things, but I couldn't think of anything suitable, and so I decided to tell Sae how the festival went down.

Blessed with clear weather and a sizable turnout, the choir festival set off to a flying start. After the opening declaration and the principal's speech, I conducted the first highlight of the day – the ensemble choir with the entire student body singing as one – which was met with a round of applause and set the tone for the whole event.

Around forty minutes in, it was time for Class 1A to give its performance. The students lined up on the stage as rehearsed and started signing *Ode to the Earth* to Yokota's piano accompaniment. The choir, which I had last heard just the day before, failed to meet my expected standard, though of course, I had no right to complain. I was a little nervous about how the surprising climax at the end would be received, but it was too late to do anything about it now. All I could do was sit still at the MC table just below the stage trying my best to listen – or rather, *not* to listen.

Then, just as the song entered its second half, right as Yokota finished her powerful and emotional piano interlude and the choir was about to start setting up the eventual climax, a loud, piercing noise sounded throughout the gymnasium.

It was such a thunderous, violent roar it could have given someone a heart attack. It was like being bombarded by the cries of hundreds of cicadas glued to a single tree, the blast all but devastating my brain. Purely by instinct, I raised my hands to cover my ears out of fear it might damage my hearing.

The sound was coming simultaneously from every single mobile phone inside the gymnasium, a sickening buzzing sound, like a mechanical drill a dentist might use when filing your teeth, piercing the air, and between each ring, a woman's voice kept repeating the word: 'Earthquake. Earthquake. Earthquake.' It was a din designed to attract maximal attention and evoke an acute sense of crisis.

The peaceful atmosphere of the choir festival fell apart, the gymnasium descending into a state of pandemonium. With the choir's performance interrupted, some students gave way to panic, while more than a couple of parents bolted outside. Within moments, the gymnasium started shaking noiselessly – though compared to the shock of the alarm, it wasn't a particularly strong tremor. The movements were so subtle, in fact, they might have gone unnoticed if not for the alert.

While the hall was gripped in the throes of confusion, the alarm, at least, had stopped before the shaking fully subsided. Once I was finally confident there was no risk of another earthquake alert assaulting my auditory senses, I remembered my duty and pulled my hands away from my ears. My heart was still racing, and the ringing in my eardrums had yet to ease, but that didn't stop me from reaching for the microphone to ask the students to reprise their performance of *Ode to the Earth*. But just before I could switch it on, I was thrown into a second state of delirium by the disturbing sound rising up from near my feet, a noise unlike anything I knew. It might not even have been a sound by that point, but the fact remained it was a type of wave unlike any I had experienced before. I had no idea how it had even come to be. I almost screamed out loud. I wanted it to stop, immediately – I *needed* it to stop. It was a *noise* that had no place anywhere on this earth.

Before I knew it, my mouth swallowed the words I should have spoken next, and I instead instructed the students to step down from the stage so the next class could take their turn. It was as if my mind and voice had been hijacked by the music.

Fortunately, there were no aftershocks, and the performers and attendees slowly regained their sense of calm. As the event's host, I wrestled with myself about how to handle the unresolved issue of Class 1A. Both as the individual in charge of the entire festival and as the students' homeroom teacher, I debated how I ought to respond to this unforeseen situation and the best timing to bring them back onto the stage. After each of the other classes completed their performances, I rehearsed lines in my head like 'Ladies and gentlemen, we will now make a slight alteration to the programme to allow Class 1A, which was interrupted earlier, to perform *Ode to the Earth* once again.' Yet each time I flipped the switch on the microphone, that unsettling *noise* echoed in my ears, robbing me of my voice and driving me mad. The greater my urgency to let the class repeat their song, the louder it grew. By the time the last class finished singing, it had grown powerful enough to drown out the audience's applause. I noticed several teachers and parents approaching me, their facial muscles moving wildly as they spoke. Perhaps they were unhappy with my moderating and had come to voice their dissatisfaction. But it didn't matter how desperate they were, I simply couldn't hear them.

'What are you saying?' I asked each face that stormed my way, but I couldn't even hear my own voice anymore. That demoralising *noise* was drowning out everything else.

At that moment, my gaze settled on the clock on the far wall. It was exactly the scheduled time for my special performance. And so, giving into the cacophony, I said: 'To close off this choir festival, we will now listen to a special piece titled *Black Monkey*, composed and performed by Mitsui Sonata.'

As I introduced myself over the microphone, the *noise* died off. I brought my equipment in from the wings and launched into a show I had spent the past six months preparing for, focusing solely on giving my best DJ performance yet.

At the end of the day, Yokota approached while I was busy tidying up in the gymnasium, cursing me in her excited, monkey-like screech. She was incredibly worked up, criticising me again and again for not letting the class redo their recital, and castigating my special performance as 'terrible music, impossible to sit through'.

'You don't care about your students' feelings, do you, Ms Mitsui?' she fumed.

I offered up no excuses or counterarguments, though what she said was only half true. I *had* considered the feelings of the students, and I believed I had made the best choice for them. I had no regrets.

This was because I knew that if I were to give Class 1A another chance to sing, the same misfortune would strike all over again. The earth would quake, shaking the gymnasium back and forth and preventing the choir from ever reaching the end. No matter what, it would keep them from raising their hands up to the heavens. Which was why I couldn't bring myself to let my dear students repeat their error. No matter how many times they tried, the result would always be the same. I had read the earth's intentions through the soles of my feet, and my intuition was never off the mark when it came to sounds.

Yokota, however, proceeded to elaborate on her unique musical theory, delivering a parting remark just as she had back in the music room not a week before: 'You're not qualified to call yourself "Sonata". You're completely blind to the human heart. Why don't you change your name to "Koala" or something?'

Listening to this still-growing girl mercilessly chide her teacher, my eyes followed the movements of the organs comprising her face. My hands reached out to touch my own corresponding muscles, pulling them, tracing their form, folding them inward. It was astonishing how great a difference existed between her organs and mine, despite the fact they looked exactly the same and were made out of the same materials. I had heard the *noise*, yet Yokota hadn't. She jumped back as I traced the contours of my own ears, her eyebrows coming together in distrust. 'What the hell are you doing?' her expression all but said. But I didn't care. I didn't try to put on my best face. I simply continued to toy with my ears until my heart stopped racing.

At some point during my account, Sae, listening on in silence, started clinging to my arm, burying her face in my sleeve. I could feel her body trembling slightly, but whether she was laughing or crying or something else was causing her to shake, I couldn't tell. Knowing her sensitive heart, she had probably sensed elements to the story I couldn't even imagine. I had known her for years by this point, but never before had we been so close. I could feel her warm breath falling on my cold arm.

'In the end, they're just monkeys in uniforms,' I said, savouring the wine in my mug. 'Tears falling, voices calling, painting me the villain, it's fucking appalling. They say I'm giving them the worst sort of teaching, that my tunes are trash, devoid of meaning. I'm sick of their preachy lines, always laying down clichés, like worn-out signs. Disrespecting pure vibes they can't see, so even if I drop dope lines, it's all debris. Deaf ears, bad vibes, their too-narrow view, I just wanna tell them to join the zoo.'

Completely by chance, a rhythm I had heard somewhere spilled from my lips, and it was the perfect fit for my present situation.

My complaints continued to pour out one after the next, and there I was aiming for Sae's slender body, her delicate skin and glossy hair, while at the same time trying to maintain some sense of rhyme. I couldn't see her face, so it was ultimately a rather one-sided conversation, but I didn't care. I let the words pour out. I didn't bother to consider the meaning behind her cryptic behaviour, and I didn't particularly care to find out. In the chaos of the moment, I asked her to lower the rent a little bit. I knew she was giving me a good discount, but seeing as I would soon be unemployed, even the smallest reduction would help. And, I insisted, I would put my instruments away and keep the house tidy. Sae said nothing in response, merely pressing her small chest tightly against my arms, trembling slightly with every breath.

As I spoke, I suddenly realised my voice seemed to have changed in timbre from how I remembered it. I hardly recognised as my own the sounds spewing out my throat and bouncing back to me from Sae's body. They couldn't be any more unlike my voice of ten years earlier, back when I had been a high-school student. My voice when talking back to my dad had been several pitches higher, sharp, and with a certain dampness to it. But now, those characteristics had all but vanished, and in their place, the notes that reached my ears were dry and deep, as if craving a certain unspecified 'something'. Yes, it was the voice of a tired woman in her late twenties. Just like how Michael Jackson's singing voice changed from his childhood to youth through to middle age, it seemed my vocal cords were changing slightly with each passing day. Perhaps my facial training exercises had hastened the effect? It occurred to me I had never really paused to listen to myself properly, but perhaps my own voice could be used to make some new kind of music. There *had* to be sounds out there suited to these new tones. But what? And so, with that thought, I squeezed my eyes shut and listened, hoping to strike on the sounds that lay ahead.

www.ingramcontent.com/pod-product-compliance
Lightning Source LLC
LaVergne TN
LVHW091137080826
845145LV00008B/2184

* 9 7 8 1 7 6 3 6 0 0 9 2 8 *